U0066631

瑞蘭國際

Focal Point Taiwan

Formosan Snapshots

用英語說
臺灣文化
浮光掠影話臺灣

國立政治大學
崔正芳（Cynthia Tsui）　編著
徐鎠（Ruth Hsu）　審訂

緣起

國立政治大學外國語文學院的治學目標之一，就是要促進對世界各地文化的了解，並透過交流與溝通，令對方也認識我國文化。所謂知己知彼，除了可消弭不必要的誤會，更能增進互相的情誼，我們從事的是一種綿密細緻的交心活動。

再者，政大同學出國交換的比率極高，每當與外國友人交流，談到本國文化時，往往會詞窮，或手邊缺少現成的外語資料，造成溝通上的不順暢，實在太可惜，因此也曾提議是否能出一本類似教材的文化叢書。這個具體想法來自斯拉夫語文學系劉心華教授，與同仁們開會討論後定案。

又，透過各種交流活動，我們發現太多外國師生來臺後都想繼續留下來，不然就是臨別依依不捨，日後總找機會續前緣，再度來臺，甚至呼朋引伴，攜家帶眷，樂不思蜀。當然，有些人學習有成，可直接閱讀中文；但也有些人仍需依靠其母語，才能明白內容。為了讓更多人認識寶島、了解臺灣，我們於是興起編纂雙語的《用外語說臺灣文化》的念頭。

而舉凡國內教授最多語種的高等教育學府，就屬國立政治大學外國語文學院，且在研究各國民情風俗上，翻譯與跨文化中心耕耘頗深，舉辦過的文康、藝文、學術活動更不勝枚舉。然而，若缺乏系統性整理，難以突顯同仁們努力的成果，於是我們藉由「教育部高教深耕計畫」，結合院內各語種本國師與外師的力量，著手九冊（英、德、法、西、俄、韓、日、土、阿）不同語言的《用外語說臺灣文化》，以外文為主，中文為輔，提供對大中華區文化，尤其是臺灣文化有興趣的愛好者參閱。

　　我們團隊花了一、兩年的時間,將累積的資料大大梳理一番,各自選出約十章精華。並透過彼此不斷地切磋、增刪、審校,並送匿名審查,終於完成這圖文並茂的系列書。也要感謝幕後無懼辛勞的瑞蘭國際出版編輯群,才令本套書更加增色。其中內容深入淺出,目的就是希望讀者易懂、易吸收,因此割愛除去某些細節,但願專家先進不吝指正,同時內文亦能博君一粲。

阮若缺
國立政治大學外國語文學院院長
於指南山麓

Preface

Upon knowing the opportunity to work with my colleagues to publish a series of books in nine different languages, introducing our homeland to foreign expatriates and visitors in Taiwan, I was truly excited about the project! The book series will serve our outbound exchange students or professionals relocated to foreign countries when they introduce Taiwan to their new friends on foreign soil.

As I began collecting materials for my book, I realized that there had been zillions of books written in English introducing Taiwan, let alone those glamourous YouTubers introducing Taiwan's pop culture and tourist spots on a daily basis. How would my book even begin to compete with those predecessors on the market? I couldn't help but wonder what approach I should take to yield a different perspective than what's already available.

I thought about the panic and uncertainty I felt when going abroad for my graduate studies in my early 20s. Those memories of cross-cultural encounters, some hilarious, some embarrassing, came flashing through my mind. I also thought about the "reverse" culture shock that I experienced when I re-entered my own culture after spending many years abroad. Not until then did I know that I was ready to talk about entering a foreign culture. Thanks to the multiple brainstorming sessions with the project faculty, I began to revisit many Taiwanese cultural practices with which I grew up.

The more topics I explored, the more ignorant I realized I had been about my homeland. The more I wrote, the more I rediscovered this place I call home. As if I were given a chance to re-live those moments in history, where the country experienced social and political turmoil, the entire writing process has been a journey for me to re-connect with my roots. Because of the reconnection, I was able to better understand and appreciate the beauty and sophistication behind many cultural practices I once took for granted.

The book is organized into nine chapters as follows:
Chapter 1 Natural Landscapes
Chapter 2 History & Population
Chapter 3 Industry & Innovations
Chapter 4 Religious Mural
Chapter 5 Holidays & Festivals
Chapter 6 Culinary Delights
Chapter 7 Social Pulse
Chapter 8 Folk Practices
Chapter 9 Arts & Entertainment

These chapters have been purposefully chosen to reflect the "traditional" Taiwan, the "tech-savvy" Taiwan, and the "gender-inclusive" Taiwan. Within each chapter, there are several short articles surrounding the chapter's theme, each offering a more in-depth view. Each piece comes with a bilingual text. The Chinese version is usually more condensed and in no way a verbatim translation of the English version. In some cases, the two versions in the same article may differ a great deal. The purpose is to provide the most relevant information under the proper bilingual contexts. Also, some historical events were described without precise citations despite painstaking efforts to double-check for accuracy. Apologies for any undetected errors or omissions, as this is not the intention. The standard pinyin Romanization with tone is used for most of the Chinese words throughout the book except for proper names of cities and places commonly known to the West, such as Taipei, Keelung, Hsinchu, which use the old Wade-Giles spelling.

Heartfelt thanks go to David Yu (游輝弘) for his generosity in granting the book to use his award-winning photographs. These photographs, taken by Mr. Yu in his prime time as a professional photographer, captured many moments in which the people of Taiwan embraced and celebrated life despite political and social unrest. These images have reminded me of the spirit and soul of the Taiwanese people that I take so much pride in. I'm deeply indebted to David for his kindness.

I also want to express gratitude to my proofreader, Ruth Hsu (徐 鎝), born and raised in the United States, who wouldn't mind my countless questions about tedious English problems. Because of her bilingual and bi-cultural background, she understood my perspectives perfectly. Her suggestions have worked wonders, for which I'm truly grateful.

Finally, if I had written this book long ago, I would have shared it with my grandmother, who didn't have a chance to visit Taiwan during her lifetime. Granny (親婆), this book is for you!

Cynthia Tsui
Mucha, Taipei
December, 2021

編著者序

　　很榮幸參與了教育部深耕計畫「用外語說臺灣文化」的團隊，分別以九個語種(英、法、德、西、俄、土、阿、日、韓語)書寫介紹臺灣文化的套書。我負責的語種是英語，當我知道這個計畫的內容時，心裡躊躇著：介紹臺灣的英語書籍簡直汗牛充棟，再加上現在國內國外的網紅名人，每天都有推陳出新介紹臺灣的英語影音資料，我的這本書究竟會有甚麼賣點？

　　經過團隊多次的腦力激盪，我們慢慢地看到這套書籍的定位，是給目前已在臺灣或欲前往臺灣工作或定居的外籍人士，一套能夠瞭解臺灣文化底蘊的書籍，不是一般的旅遊叢書，而是從社會、歷史、民俗、族群等角度切入的文化觀察。另一群鎖定的讀者則是欲出國深造或工作的臺灣本地人，可以藉由這套書籍，將臺灣的豐富文化介紹給不同國家的朋友。

　　在確定了這套書的定位之後，團隊也確信多元語種將是這套書最重要的特點之一，如果僅因市面上已經充滿介紹臺灣的英語書籍，就打退堂鼓、獨缺了英語的版本，那套書的國際性就會因此打折扣，畢竟英語仍然是目前國際的通用語言。但是我既沒有史詩級的文筆，也沒有網紅級的風采，僅僅為本套書最佳綠葉的陪襯角色，懷抱著這樣的心情，我開始了我的書寫過程。

　　從蒐集資料、篩選主題、閱讀撰寫的過程中，我才驚覺我對我生長的這塊土地竟是如此無知。可能在歷史社會課本中讀過的反清復明鄭成功、荷蘭日據時代、原住民的遷徙等，背後有太多的先民血淚與社會動盪，都不曾在我年輕時的腦海中駐足，而是要到了步入中年的我，在經過了許多年異鄉求學的洗禮，再回到家鄉後，才能看到家鄉的斑斕過去，也才知道多年來家鄉早已脫胎換骨，擺脫了滄桑的過往，開創了全新的局面。

本書共囊括了九個章節如下：

第一章 地理景觀

第二章 歷史與人口

第三章 產業科技脈動

第四章 宗教信仰

第五章 節慶與祭典

第六章 飲食文化

第七章 社會脈動

第八章 民間習俗

第九章 藝術與休閒

　　主題的選擇，除了重要節慶、歷史地理、飲食文化等傳統題材，也囊括了臺灣近幾年在同婚及性別平權上獲得世界矚目的發展，在科技文創上的日新月異，還有與國際接軌的環保政策。這些主題的探討，是想讓讀者一窺臺灣社會源源不斷的演化力與包容力，也讓本書展現與時俱進的特色。

　　每個章節各有數篇短文，圍繞章節的主題發展。每篇文章都有中、英語的敘述，但不是逐句翻譯，英語版是文章主軸，中文版則主精簡，僅提供文章摘要。書中提及的歷史事件，有些沒有列文獻出處，但已盡可能以非歷史學家的身份來考據。文中大部分使用漢語拼音系統（Pinyin），除了慣用的地名或人名，才會使用韋傑士拼音系統（Wade-Giles）。

　　要特別感謝游輝弘先生，慷慨提供他攝影生涯中得獎的多張照片：雲門舞集、媽祖出巡、王船祭典、平溪天燈的影像，捕捉了臺灣人民的日常，即便在時代變遷的動盪中，也從不曾停止對生命的禮讚。很感謝這些照片為此書的文字更添光彩。另外要感謝我的潤稿人徐鎔女士，她在美國出生、成長、工作，後來回到臺灣，因為她的跨文化素養，讓我的文字更洗鍊道地，並精準地傳達了我的想法，她是這本書背後的魔術師！

因為書寫家鄉，讓我重新認識家鄉的蛻變；因為曾是遊子，讓我體會身在臺灣的遊子心情。在書寫過程中，許多幼時回憶及異鄉片段湧上心頭，曾經混沌的國家民族認同感，此刻竟了了分明，原來我也在此書的撰寫過程中找到了回家的路。

崔正芳

崔正芳寫於指南山麓
110.12.2

Table of Contents 目次

Chapter 1

第一單元

Natural Landscapes
地理景觀

1.1 地理位置

　　臺灣地處東亞，介於菲律賓與日本之間，葡萄牙人在 16 世紀時來到了這個島嶼，驚豔於它的草木蒼翠，便將它命名為「福爾摩沙」，意思是「美麗之島」，從此西方國家就經常以此稱呼臺灣。臺灣其實是由一個大島及其他幾個小離島組成的，包括本島、澎湖、金門、馬祖、綠島、蘭嶼、小琉球，總領土面積 35,886 平方公里，相當於荷蘭的國土大小。

　　中央山脈是臺灣島內的山脈主線，其中最高的玉山，也是東北亞最高的山脈。中央山脈西側多平原，東側則多為山谷與海岸礁石的地形，因為有高山，成就了許多溪谷地形，聞名中外的太魯閣峽谷，即是一例。又因為有遼闊的大平原，才能生產豐饒的農作物。雖然臺灣國土面積很小，但地形豐富多變化，造就了很多美麗的自然景觀與生態。

Taiwan seen at night from the space

1.1 Geography

● ●

Taiwan is an island country located in East Asia between the Philippines and Japan. It consists of the main island and several other smaller islands. In 1544, Portuguese sailors first christened the main island *Formosa*, or "beautiful island" in Portuguese, when they first discovered the island and were amazed by its landscapes and scenery. The main island measures 394 kilometers (245 miles) long and 144 km (89 miles) wide. In addition to the main island, there are several smaller islands including: Penghu Archipelago, Kinmen and Matsu Islands that are to the west in the Taiwan Strait, Green Island and Orchid Island that are to the east in the Pacific Ocean, and a tiny islet of Xiaoliuqiu to the southwest of the main island. Taiwan's total land area is 35,886 km^2 (13,856 sq mi), an area comparable to the Netherlands.

The main island, having the largest number and density of high mountains globally, has 286 mountain summits over 3,000 meters (9,800 ft) above sea level. The Central Mountain Range is the principal mountain range that stretches 340 kilometers from the north to the south. The highest peak in the range is Mount Jade (elevation 3,952 meters), which is also the highest mountain in Northeast Asia. Because of the tallest peak, Taiwan also ranks as the world's fourth-highest island.

The east side of the Central Mountain Range is abundant with mountainous slopes and rocky terrain. Taroko Gorge, one of the national parks, is situated in the steep mountains near the east coast of Taiwan. Vast plains lie on

Moutain Jade in Yushan National Park

the west side of the mountain range where the country's rice and wheat are grown, and it is also where most of the population reside. Northern Taiwan also sits a group of extinct or dormant volcanos such as Mount Guanyin and Mount Datun, making the nearby areas natural spots for hot springs. Outlying islands such as Green Island, Orchid Island, and Penghu Archipelago are also remnants of extinct volcanos. Despite its small geographical size, Taiwan boasts various geographical features, including majestic mountains, rocky and sandy beaches, wide-stretching plains, and serene lakes amidst mountainous areas.

1.2 氣候

　　臺灣居於熱帶與亞熱帶之間，北迴歸線在島嶼的中央通過，北半部是亞熱帶氣候，南半部則是熱帶氣候。四季之中，夏天及冬天的溫度變化較明顯，夏天可以達到攝氏 37 度（華式 98.6 度）的高溫，冬天最冷則會降到攝氏 10 度以下（華式 40 度）。雖然沒有四季分明的氣候，但春天及秋天仍有別於夏、冬兩季的酷熱與嚴寒，氣候宜人，是最適合出遊賞花踏青的季節。

Nanhu Mountain

1.2 Climate

The climate in Taiwan is usually warm and rainy. Annual rainfall in Taiwan is around 2,500 millimeters (100 inches). The Tropic of Cancer passes through the center of the main island, dividing Taiwan into a tropical climate in the southern region and a subtropical climate in the northern and central regions. The four seasons are not as clearly demarcated. Summer is usually hot and humid, with temperatures reaching as high as 37 degrees Celsius (98.6 degrees Fahrenheit) throughout the months of July and August. It is a great time to do outdoor and water activities. Sunglasses, hats, and sunscreen are strongly recommended.

Tropic of Cancer landmarker in Hualien

From July to October is the typhoon season. These tropical cyclones usually form within the western Pacific Ocean and bring torrential rains and strong winds that can cause mudslides, floods, and substantial damage. Most Taiwanese have experienced power outages during a typhoon night and are well prepared with the necessary supplies ahead of time.

In autumn, generally from September to October, the weather is cool and pleasant, perfect for hiking and other outdoor activities, especially when the humidity is not as high. Colorful autumn foliage does not happen as intensely in Taiwan as the temperatures do not drop significantly during the fall season. But in national parks at higher elevations such as Yushan National Park, leaves from trees change their hues more reliably and add to the charm of autumn foliage.

Although it could be sweltering during summer in Taiwan, winters can be bitterly cold. In northern Taiwan, a subtropical zone, temperatures can drop to single digits in Celsius degrees (35 ~ 50 degrees Fahrenheit) during winter. In the mountainous areas, there is occasional snow recorded between January and February months. Steady rainfall in northern Taiwan during winter makes the humidity rise again, which adds to the coldness's chill factor. Nevertheless, the southern part of Taiwan, a tropical zone, remains mostly sunny during the winter. Because most households in Taiwan are not built with central heating systems, indoor spaces during winter can get as cold as outdoor ones.

Spring marks another pleasant season in Taiwan. From March to May, trees sprout and flowers blossom everywhere on the island. People can spot cherry blossoms in the front yards of residences inside the cities or rural areas. Due to its tropical marine climate, Taiwan also boasts a vast array of flora present on the island, where approximately 4000 species of vascular plants consider as home.

Alocasia fields in Taipei

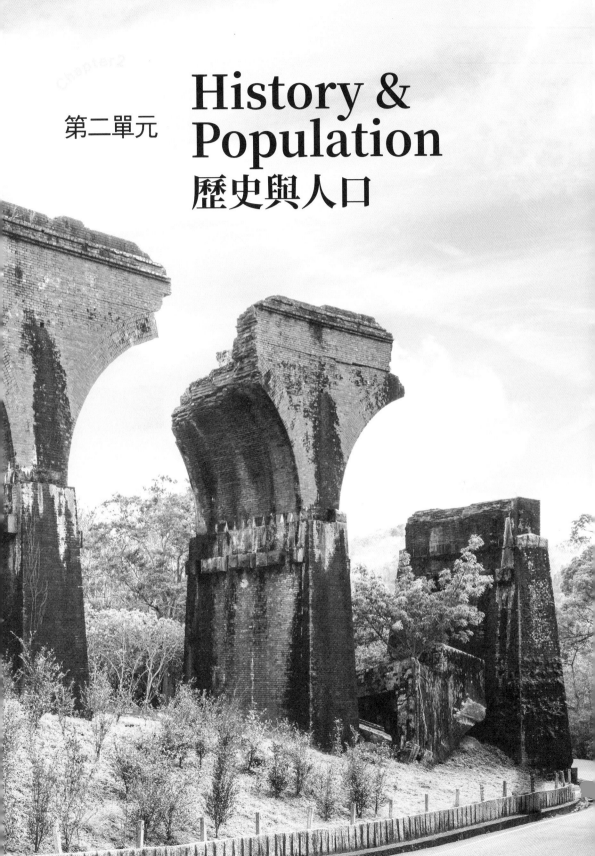

第二單元

History & Population
歷史與人口

2.1 殖民時期的歷史回顧

　　自 17 世紀起，臺灣便開始經歷許多外來勢力的統治。1624 年，荷蘭人欲以澎湖為基地，與日本通商，始於臺灣南部登陸。二年後，西班牙人則為了與南太平洋的菲律賓進行區域合作，並抗衡荷蘭人在南臺灣的勢力，而從臺灣北部登陸。但西班牙的統治在 16 年後即告終止。1642 年，荷蘭人攻下西人在北臺灣的最後一座城池，西班牙的勢力從此退出。總和荷蘭人在臺近 40 年的殖民期間，在臺南地區留下許多建樹。直至 1662 年，明朝的將領鄭成功來到臺灣，驅逐了荷蘭人的勢力，建立了他自己的王朝。

　　鄭成功又稱「國姓爺」，在他的帶領下，人民安居樂業，社會繁榮，人民因此感念他，現在臺南的國立成功大學、鄭成功廟，還有街道名稱等，皆是為了紀念他而以他的名字命名的。但好景不常，1683 年，清朝的武力又擊潰了鄭成功的勢力，將臺灣納入清朝的疆土。

　　1895 年，清朝在中日甲午戰爭戰敗後，將臺灣割讓給日本，正式開始日本在臺灣 50 年的殖民統治。日本在臺期間設立銀行、學校、醫院，又興建鐵路、公路等設施，為臺灣的基礎建設打下根基，但他們殖民當時的嚴刑峻法，對臺灣人民的高壓統治，仍然引發了許多流血衝突事件。1945 年，日本在第二次世界大戰宣布戰敗，退出臺灣，正式結束對臺灣的統治。

　　經過幾個世紀的外來勢力統治，臺灣終於在 1996 年行使首度的民選總統，開啟政治史上的新頁。過去的外力介入，都是孕育臺灣的養分，也因為如此，才成就了臺灣現今多元包容的社會。

2.1 Foreign Powers

Foreign influence on Taiwan took place as early as during the Age of Exploration when Portuguese sailors arrived and were impressed by the island's natural scenery. They called it "Ilha Formosa" – beautiful island in Portuguese, hence granting the island country its nickname in the West – Formosa.

In 1624, the Dutch occupied the island and ruled for nearly four decades (Liu, 2009). They wanted to establish a trading post on the outskirt Penghu Archipelago so they could trade with Japan. They built a stronghold in the southern part of Taiwan, which is now Anping, Tainan. In 1626, another foreign power, the Spanish Empire, landed on the shores of northern Taiwan and ruled for 16 years. The colony was maintained to protect Spain's regional trade with the Philippines against the Dutch base in southern Taiwan; however, the Spanish settlement was short-lived. In 1642, the Dutch took over the last Spanish fortress and claimed control over much of the island. It was during the Dutch colonization of Taiwan when the migration of settlers from Fujian, China, was initiated to extend Dutch trading power. However, the Dutch were defeated, after a year-long battle, and expelled from the island in 1662 by a Chinese general named Zheng Chenggong (鄭成功), more commonly known as Koxinga (國姓爺).

Koxinga was a general-in-exile loyal to the Ming emperor[1]. He retreated to

---

1. The Ming Dynasty (1368 ~ 1644) precedes the Qing Dynasty (1644 ~ 1912) in the imperial history of China.

Taiwan as the Qing forces had claimed territories in China and forced the last Ming emperor to flee and eventually commit suicide. Knowing that the dynasty to which he swore allegiance no longer existed, Koxinga continued to fight the Qing forces and, later, established the Kingdom of Tungning in present-day Tainan from 1661 to 1683. To this day, he is still remembered for his charismatic leadership and accredited for replacing Dutch colonial rule with a more modern political system in Taiwan. As such, statues of Koxinga, hundreds of temples and schools, including a university, National Cheng Kung University, are named after him for his legacy and association with the idea of Taiwanese independence.

In 1683, Koxinga's forces were defeated by the Qing dynasty, officially making Taiwan part of the Qing Empire. In 1895, the Qing lost in the Sino-Japanese War and had to cede the island to the Empire of Japan. The Japanese rule of Taiwan was marked by rapid economic and social development. They built infrastructure, including roads and railway tracks, and set up banks, schools, and hospitals. Despite their contribution to the modernization of the island, the Japanese governors were harsh to Taiwan's inhabitants, often resulting in deadly conflicts. After 50 years of occupation, they were defeated in World War II and forced to leave the island.

Throughout the colonial periods, these foreign powers exerted their influence on the development of the island in dimensions and, to a great extent, helped Taiwan to build its resilience and to embrace diversity.

2.2 人口組成與變遷

臺灣二千三百萬的人口中涵蓋了各種族群，其中 70% 是所謂的河洛人，他們是 17、18 世紀時即從中國的福建省遷徙到臺灣的早期移民的後代。另外 13% 的人口是客家人，他們分別來自中國的數個省份，並逐漸往南方省份遷徙，最後抵達臺灣，因為他們不斷做為「旅人」、「客人」般的遷徙歷史，而被稱為「客家人」，許多客家人更遠甚至遷徙到東南亞、非洲各個國家。第三大族群是佔 13% 的「外省人」，這是在 1949 年隨著蔣介石的軍隊一起來臺灣的中國各省的軍旅人口的後代，相較於早年即來臺的河洛人與客家人，外省人來臺的時間更晚。除了這三大族群外，還有 2% 的原住民人口，雖然佔總人口數不多，他們卻是比前三大族群都更早就居住在島上的南島語系民族，目前在臺灣的這些原住民共有 16 個不同的部落，各自有不同的族語及傳統。近 20 年來，臺灣又增加了最新的族群，他們是經過通婚或工作，自東南亞移民到臺灣的新移民，大約有 57 萬人，已經佔總人口比例 2.4%，成為臺灣的第五大人口族群。

2.2 Population

The population in Taiwan is around 23 million people, among which 70% identify as Hoklo, 13% as Hakka, 13% as Mainlanders, and 2% as indigenous people. The Hoklo people are descendants of Han people initially from the southern province of China, Fujian. They made their way to Taiwan in the 17th and 18th centuries and are now the biggest ethnic group in Taiwan.

The next leading ethnic group is the Hakka people, who were thought to have originally come from the northern provinces of China and gradually migrated to southern China. They eventually moved and settled in Taiwan. The Chinese characters of Hakka literally mean "guest" or "traveler." Their skillful migration mobility and adaptability may explain why there are Hakka people in Taiwan and throughout Southeast Asia and even South Africa. There is a Hakka adage: "Wherever there is sunshine, there are Chinese; wherever there are Chinese, there are Hakka." Hakka people have managed to keep their own language and customs alive for generations, long after they migrated and settled in Taiwan.

Another 13 percent of the population in Taiwan are those who arrived in Taiwan with Chiang Kai-shek's Nationalist Party when the Communist Party took control of mainland China in 1949. This group, along with their descendants, are often referred to as the Mainlanders. Those who came with the Nationalist Party in 1949 were from different provinces in China and spoke different dialects. Their children, however, growing up in Taiwan, mostly do not learn to speak their hometown dialects.

The remaining 2 percent of the population in Taiwan are the indigenous people who are said to have lived on the island for approximately 5,500 years. These Taiwanese aborigines are Austronesian peoples, with linguistic and genetic ties to other Austronesian peoples. Today, there are 16 tribes, each with its distinct language and customs. The 16 officially recognized indigenous tribes in Taiwan are Amis (阿美族), Atayal (泰雅族), Bunun (布農族), Kanakanavu (卡那卡那富族), Kavalan (噶瑪蘭族), Paiwan (排灣族), Puyuma (卑南族), Rukai (魯凱族), Saisiyat (賽夏族), Saaroa (拉阿魯哇族), Sakizaya (撒奇萊雅族), Seediq (賽德克族), Tao/Yami (達悟族), Thao (邵族), Truku (太魯閣族), Tsou (鄒族). There are some aboriginal groups, up to 26,000 indigenous people, yet to be formally identified and classified. Some smaller tribes, unfortunately, have become extinct before being recognized.

In recent decades, Taiwan has embraced another new group of immigrants from Southeast Asia. Since the Council of Labor Affairs approved foreign labor employment in 1999, many foreign nationals have come to work in Taiwan. Through labor migration and interethnic marriage, people from Cambodia, Indonesia, Laos, the Philippines, Thailand, and Vietnam have joined the workforce or built their own families in Taiwan. They make up 2% strong of the total population. Today, there are approximately 570,000 foreign residents in Taiwan, many of whom have naturalized as citizens and brought new perspectives and customs to Taiwan's society and communities.

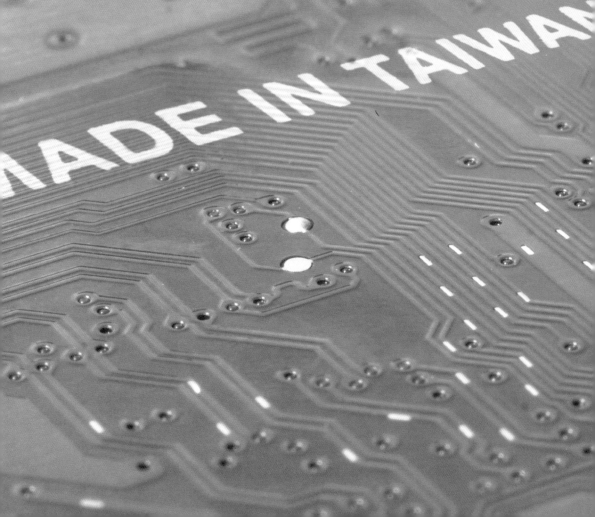

Industry & Innovations

產業科技脈動

3.1 蛻變的經濟體

臺灣的經濟發展與當時的政治社會變遷息息相關，大致可分為以下七個階段：

第一階段（1950s）：二次大戰及日據殖民時期結束後的社會重建，推動土地改革以確保糧產自給自足，農產食品為代表性產業。

第二階段（1960s）：勞力密集的加工出口產業，紡織為代表性產業。

第三階段（1970s）：改善基礎建設，推動十大建設，設置科學園區，石化鋼鐵為代表性產業。

第四階段（1980s）：經濟自由化，推動資訊工業發展，晉升亞洲四小龍之列，資訊為代表性產業。

第五階段（1990s）：產業升級，推動亞太營運中心，成為亞太地區的經濟樞紐，半導體為代表性產業。

第六階段（2000s）：創新研發，推動知識經濟，加入世界貿易組織，服務業及高產值傳統產業為代表性產業。

第七階段（2010至今）：數位家園，培植新興產業及鼓勵個人創業，推動國際接軌與南向政策，數位科技及環保為代表性產業。

3.1 Economic Transformation

Taiwan's economic development has evolved over time in accordance with its political and social development. In general, there are a total of seven stages to describe the changes to the economy. The first stage began in the 1950s, in which postwar reconstruction after Japanese colonial rule to restore social stability was the top priority. In particular, food production to ensure self-sufficiency was the chief goal of the government policy. Implementation of land reform to encourage agricultural production as a stabilization of food prices was one of the strategic measures. The government also nurtured labor-intensive and import-substitution industries that would, in time, help reduce the trade deficit.

Due to the labor-intensive industry built in the 1950s, the economy shifted to a labor-intensive, export-oriented structure in the 1960s, when the second stage – Expansion of Light Industry Exports – began. During this stage, the government established export processing zones to encourage foreign investments. At the time, Taiwan's low-cost labor successfully attracted a great number of investors and enjoyed a rapid growth of exports in international markets while riding the waves with the thriving world economy.

By the end of the 1960s, accelerated export expansion had led to strong domestic demand for machinery equipment and intermediate raw materials. Promotion of domestic substitutes for imported raw materials helped upgrade the industrial structure and reduced its dependence on foreign supplies of essential goods. The 1970s marked the third economic development stage during which import substitution and infrastructure improvement took place. It was also in this period that the government initiated the Ten New Major Construction Projects which enhanced capital-intensive industries in producing intermediate goods such as steel and chemicals.

In the 1980s, Taiwan adopted economic liberalization and internationalization as new principles to develop capital- and technology-intensive industries in electronics, machinery, and information technology. It was during this fourth stage that Taiwan's trade surplus continued to boom, and abundant capital was utilized to bring market forces into full play. The export-driven policy and rapid industrialization had made Taiwan one of the Four Asian Tigers, along with Hong Kong, Singapore, and South Korea, to create the Asian Miracle with their flourishing economic growth (Severns, 2021).

The fifth stage initiated in the 1990s during which Taiwan's IT industry took off. The labor-intensive industries from earlier decades had gradually transformed the island from a "toy kingdom" into an "IT kingdom." IT products such as monitors, motherboards, and scanners manufactured in Taiwan claimed over 50% of the world market – making Taiwan an essential link in the global hi-tech industry. In 1994, the government launched the Twelve Major Construction Projects aimed at making Taiwan an Asia-Pacific Regional Operations Center (APROC).

In the 2000s, the sixth stage, the pursuit of the knowledge economy and environmental sustainability earmarked the core value of the stage.

Development of semiconductor, image display, biotechnology, and digital content industries accelerated Taiwan's economic transformation. On January 1, 2002, Taiwan formally joined the World Trade Organization (WTO) and started repositioning its economy within the international trade community. The world had also witnessed Taiwan withstand the financial crisis in 2008, which is testimony to Taiwan's industrial strengths.

The 2010s began the seventh stage, the most recent stage, where industrial innovation and global linkage have been the core values so far. The government has launched the *i-Taiwan 12 Projects* (Cabinet approves budget for 'i-Taiwan 12' projects, 2009), designed to promote emerging industries, such as biotechnology, green energy, medical care, cloud computing, electric vehicles, and patent commercialization. As for global linkage, trade laws and regulations have been amended and, in some cases, relaxed to promote economic liberalization aiming at enhancing Taiwan's global logistics capabilities. The New Southbound Policy invigorates connections with the Southeast Asian countries. At the same time, liberalization boosts Taiwan's economic vitality and autonomy.

Over the past half-century, Taiwan has evolved from an agricultural society to a leading player in the global Information and Communication Technology (ICT) industry. Taiwan Semiconductor Manufacturing Company (TSMC) 台積電 is the world's largest independent semiconductor foundry with a worldwide capacity of about 13 million 300mm equivalent wafers each year, making chips for such customers Apple and Huawei, not to mention car manufacturers. Between 1952 and 2009, Taiwan's per capita income rose from US$213 to US$16,353; its GDP from US$1.7 billion to US$377 billion; and its foreign trade from US$303 million to US$378 billion (R.O.C. Council for Economic Planning and Development, 2010). Over the past decades, Taiwan has earned a vital role in the global ICT supply chain, fulfilling its vision of building the small island country into a technological giant.

3.2 臺北 101 大樓

臺北 101 大樓在 2004 到 2010 年間，登上了世界第一高樓的寶座。樓高 508 公尺，在地震與颱風頻傳的臺灣，這棟建築的設計是經過一番苦心的。在安全性上，設計了一個阻尼器，以因應颱風或高樓強風帶來的柱體搖晃。在主結構體中的八根巨柱鋼筋，其雙管結構的鋼筋讓大樓的抗震性，安然通過了完工前正巧發生的大地震考驗。通往觀景台的高速電梯，也曾創下世界最快的金氏世界紀錄。

Taipei 101 Building

樓高 101 層，乃基於 100 的完美數字，再更上層樓的意涵。同樣地在建築的外觀上，每八層樓就自成一單位，連續八個單位組成的樓塔部分，是因為「八」對華人來說是一個吉祥的數字，連續八次的八層樓就代表了順順利利、大吉大利。另外，節節高升的外觀也是取自竹子的意象，象徵大樓帶來步步高升的商業活動與運勢。樓塔與樓底座的交接處，每側都有一個古錢幣的圖騰，代表財運滾滾、旺盛繁榮。

登上大樓內的觀景台可一覽臺北市的風貌，是國際觀光客的最愛。除了是臺灣的地標，每逢跨年夜，臺北 101 大樓的煙火表演，已經成為各國際媒體捕捉的焦點，為臺灣的能見度更添一美麗新頁。

3.2 Taipei 101

For a six-year period from 2004 to 2010, the Taipei 101 building held the record of the tallest building in the world. It took five years to complete the construction of the building. Upon completion, thousands of tourists from around the world, and locals alike, came flocking in to see the skyscraper. As the name of the building implies, there are a total of 101 floors. The number symbolizes exceptional perfection as 100 is considered a traditional number of perfection. Adding one to the number 100 makes it beyond excellence. Standing at 508 meters (1667 feet) tall, Taipei 101 is designed not only to stand for Taipei, but also an acronym – Technology, Art, Innovation, People, Environment, and Identity (Rodgers, 2019).

Although the building is soon challenged and surpassed by other taller structures globally, it still enjoys many extraordinary features, including the high-speed pressurized elevators that claimed the Guinness Record in 2004. It takes only 37 seconds to reach the observatory on the 89th floor. These elevators are equipped with atmospheric controls to give passengers a ride without causing physical discomfort, for example, ear-popping. However, it was a bold idea to construct a building of this height on an island prone to earthquakes and typhoons. The design team, headed by C. Y. Lee & Partners, acutely aware of the geographical limitations, wanted to create a structurally sound and architecturally beautiful masterpiece.

A 660-ton damper has been installed hanging between the 87th floor and the 92nd floor to counterbalance the strong winds. It allows the building the

City of Taipei at sunset

flexibility to withstand gusty winds up to 134 miles per hour. The damper also swings freely to offset the building's movement, incidentally allowing the building to pass a real-life test when Taipei experienced a 6.8-magnitude earthquake in 2002 while the tower was still under construction (Rodgers, 2019).

In addition to the structural safety measures, the building is rich in its architectural beauty. The outline of Taipei 101 resembles a bamboo stalk, which signifies strength, growth, and promotion in traditional Chinese and Taiwanese cultures. The image of the bamboo reaching skyward symbolizes the vibrancy brought by the building. Some visitors jokingly comment that the building looks more like a stack of Chinese food take-out boxes. A closer look will reveal that the main tower consists of eight eight-floor sections, each rising up resembling a massive pagoda. The number eight is considered in many Asian cultures a lucky number. A repetition of eight floors repeated eight times within the same building signifies good fortune and abundance. Connecting the main tower and the pedestal are four discs on each side of the building representing coins – a symbol of prosperity.

A circle-shaped park at the base of the building makes the structure function as a giant sundial. The tower itself will cast its shadow during the afternoon hours on the circular park, which acts as the face of the sundial. The tower's shadow will mark the afternoon hours on the circular park for occupants inside the building to see. Along with the sculptures and garden plantation, the park is meant to echo the feng shui philosophy.

Currently, the building houses a shopping mall, corporate offices, restaurants, and observation decks, with an indoor one on the 89th floor and an outdoor one on the 91st floor. The highest indoor observatory is on the top (101st) floor at the height of 1,437 feet (438 meters). However, this observatory is not open to the public and remains part of an exclusive VIP club.

At the time of its completion in 2004, Taipei 101 captured the world's spotlight with its height, technological breakthroughs, and innovative design. Despite losing the crown to Dubai's Burj Khalifa in 2010, Taipei 101 remains a significant landmark in Taiwan and one of the must-sees for the New Year's fireworks.

Taipei 101 Building at night

3.3 蘭花王國

　　臺灣因為年均溫在攝氏 20～25 度，濕度及天然環境皆適合蘭花的生長，原生種的蘭花即種類繁多，種植蘭花已有 100 年的歷史。近二十年來，藉由培育術的演進，積極開發出的新品種蝴蝶蘭，已經在國際上嶄露頭角，每年光是蝴蝶蘭的外銷，已為臺灣帶來極高的產值，可謂是外銷的主力旗艦商品之一，除了開花株的蝴蝶蘭，國際市場對種苗、成長株的需求也倚賴臺灣的供應鏈。臺灣蝴蝶蘭外銷的優勢在於源源不斷開發的新品種，但每一蘭株的培育皆曠日

Phalaenopsis Black Flower

廢時，有時前後可長達十年。目前臺灣是全世界最重要的蝴蝶蘭出口國，能夠有今天的亮眼成績，都是蘭農一步一腳印耕耘出的天地，也成就了臺灣「蘭花王國」的美譽。

3.3 World Class Orchid Industry

Taiwan has won its reputation as the Kingdom of Orchids by exporting the best variety of orchids to 36 countries in North America, Europe, and South Africa (Lu and Cheng, 2015). In 2004, Taiwan hosted the 8th Asia-Pacific Orchid Conference and attracted a lot of international attention. Since then, the Taiwan Orchid Growers Association has been hosting the "Taiwan International Orchid Show (TIOS)" every year. In 2019, the number of participating countries grew nearly four-fold since 2005; the annual export value grew nearly six-fold from US$23 million to US$130 million.

Taiwan's orchid species are abundant due to its diverse landscapes. It has been growing orchids for a hundred years and only in recent decades projected itself as an export-oriented orchid industry. According to the statistics by Taiwan's Council of Agriculture, the total flower export volume in 2018 was US$209.72 million, of which 92 percent (US$192.12 million) was from the export of orchids. Taiwanese orchid growers can breed new indigenous orchids. The success of breeding the indigenous phalaenopsis (moth orchid) species proves that Taiwan's agricultural skills are up to speed to compete in the international arena. The Netherlands, another key player in the global orchid industry, introduced the same orchid species to the market only eight years ago and became an instant hit.

The battle to vie for the world's leading orchid exporter hasn't been easy. Taiwan continues to breed novelty orchid species. The breeding process begins by taking two different orchid varieties to grow a hybrid, which normally takes one year to 18 months to produce flowers. Then comes a three-year period to test its growth and flowering stability, during which more than 3000 plants would be propagated for plant tissue culture. Following another two years to test the market by sending samples of the hybrid to customers, orchid growers would finally decide whether to keep the novelty species or not. The entire breeding cycle from inception to mass production could take up to a decade to complete. The reality is, however, that the market typically responds well to a mere five percent of all the newly bred orchids, allowing growers to proceed to the mass production stage. The rest of the breeds, unfortunately, will be discontinued.

Taiwan has the ideal weather and humidity to grow orchids. Phalaenopsis is the most popular orchid among all native species. In Greek, "Phalaen" means "butterfly" and opsis means "looking like." The elegant, butterfly-shaped petals have earned it the title Queen of the Orchids. Despite a painstaking breeding process for each novelty species, orchid growers in Taiwan continue to experiment with innovative breeds. In fact, Taiwan's strengths are its diversity of orchids and advanced cultivation technologies.

Currently, the United States, Japan, and the European Union are the top three destinations for Taiwan's orchid exports. Although Europe is currently the world's largest market for orchids, the Netherlands has its market cornered. While Taiwan boasts many orchid varieties, the Dutch have the marketing lead in Europe. Several Taiwanese orchid growers thus came up with the

Phalaenopsis Princess Anne

Phalaenopsis Yellow Flower

Phalaenopsis Gukeng Beauty

strategy to work with their counterparts in the Netherlands. By granting the Dutch orchid marketers to sell Taiwanese orchid varieties with a royalty fee, Taiwanese breeders can utilize Dutch influence to penetrate and test the European market. This breakthrough is just among the many challenges facing Taiwanese orchid growers. Although there are still many hurdles to overcome, Taiwan's orchid industry has made an impressive take-off in the world race with its ever-thriving "butterfly" adventure.

3.4 中醫與中藥

　　中醫的理念認為人體就是一個小宇宙，除了肌肉、骨骼、內臟、血液，還有精、氣、神、穴道的存在，若體內的平衡被打亂，就會有疾病的出現，以及各種身體的症狀，但中醫的醫治，並非在減輕症狀或移除病兆，而是將身體的平衡再找回來，運用身體的自癒力來幫助身體回復平衡就是中醫的基本概念。

　　中醫的治療方式有中藥、針灸、按摩。中藥來自於千百種藥草的配方，以及某些動物的部位，但因為某些動物已因過度狩獵或盜獵而瀕臨絕種，所以近年來許多中醫也開始使用替代藥方，避免開立動物配方，以保護這些動物的生存權。針灸則是中醫歷久彌新的治療方式，因為療效溫和漸進，許多西方研究也漸漸開始證實針灸的療效，讓針灸成為病人可選擇的另類醫療方案之一。最後，中醫也根據人體內的經脈穴道，運用按摩推拿的方式來促進血液循環，以舒緩肌肉疼痛或協助身體深層放鬆。

　　中醫在臺灣的醫療體系裡與西醫並駕齊驅，有專屬的中醫醫療院所，許多中醫師也會自行設立診所開業。近年來有些大型西醫院，亦增設中醫部門的門診。

Chinese herbal medicine ingredients

3.4 Traditional Chinese Medicine

Traditional Chinese Medicine (TCM) is a health care discipline that originated in China over three thousand years ago and is still widely practiced in Taiwan as an alternative medical approach. TCM views the human body as a mini-universe in which illnesses will occur when any part of the body is unbalanced. The imbalance can manifest itself through symptoms such as aches, swelling, or fever; however, the body parts where these symptoms occur are not necessarily the origins of the problem. Treatments or prescriptions by TCM are not meant to tackle the symptoms but to restore the body to a balanced state.

In Taoist terms, Yin and Yang (陰、陽) are the two opposite forces in any existence of the universe and can be embodied by contrasts such as cold vs. hot, strong vs. weak, or fast vs. slow. Yin represents qualities that are more implicit, understated, descent, and soft, whereas Yang represents

Pulse diagnosis

Moxibustion therapy

qualities that are more explicit, highlighted, ascent, and strong. Yin and Yang, however, need each other to reach a balance. Illness happens when the forces of Yin and Yang inside a human body do not co-exist in harmony. Any deficiency or excess in Yin or Yang also can tip the balance.

Regarding diagnostic techniques, Western medicine uses a range of procedures such as checking the body temperature, taking blood pressure, and analyzing a blood sample to make diagnoses. Similarly, TCM relies on diagnostic procedures such as checking the pulse, studying the color of the tongue, detecting the smell of the breath, observing the face, and listening to the patient's voice before reaching a diagnostic conclusion. In fact, these procedures reflect the four vital diagnostic techniques commonly used in TCM: inspection, auscultation, olfaction, and palpation (望、聞、問、切).

Upon making a diagnosis, TCM practitioners use a combination of treatments, including herbal medicine, acupuncture, and massage. Herbal medicine comes from dried roots of plants found to be therapeutic. TCM employs approximately 1000 plants as the base of herbal medicine. Each plant has a different healing power. An appropriate combination of herbs and plants can work together to create a collective healing effect beyond herbs taken individually. Traditionally, some animal parts from tigers, rhinoceros, black bears, and seahorses were also included in the TCM practice. However, most, if not all, TCM practitioners in Taiwan now avoid giving prescriptions containing animal additives due to animal conservation efforts and illegal poaching.

Acupuncture is based on understanding a human body's vitality, called

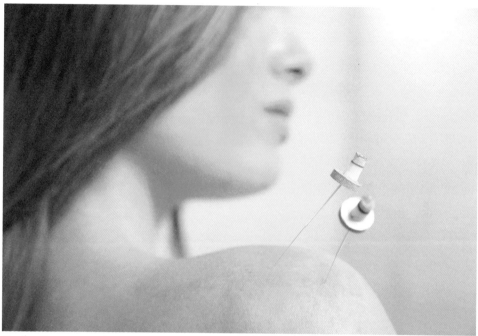

Moxibustion acupuncture

"qì" (氣), which literally means vital breath. This life force runs through different meridians of the body and connects organs, veins, and nerves holistically. If this energy network is somehow blocked, which would lead to disease, acupuncture would be able to clear the blockage and allow the vital breath to run through again. Specifically, thin needles are inserted into meridian points to stimulate the flow of qì, thereby clearing its way through various channels. Sometimes acupuncture goes along with moxibustion, which involves burning herbs at the tip of a needle to alleviate blockage. Finally, massage, also called acupressure, is often recommended by TCM practitioners to allow maximum body relaxation.

Walking into a traditional Chinese medicine pharmacy can be an eye-opening experience for a Westerner. A wall of cabinets with hundreds of drawers containing different kinds of dried herbs or animal specimens, a pharmacist would reach into several drawers and weigh each ingredient according to the prescription before wrapping each dosage. Patients then bring home the medication and boil in hot water for hours until the broth reduces to the correct consistency. Drink only the broth and toss the residue of the ingredients. In recent years, powder-based Chinese medication, much like pills and capsules in Western medicine, has been invented as an answer to the prayers for a more user-friendly consumption method. It is also easier to store at room temperature and to carry around in small dosages. In general, prescriptions in broth are more potent and cost more due to the lengthy production process, whereas those in powder form are milder and less expensive. Both forms are readily available for patients to choose from at their convenience. For decades, TCM has been a legitimate alternative health care approach in Taiwan and is receiving more recognition worldwide these days.

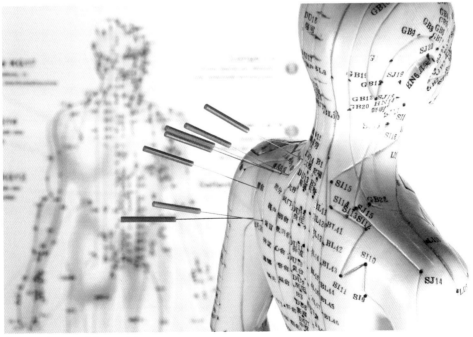

Acupuncture meridian points

3.5 交通號誌的故事

在臺灣的任何一個街頭角落，準備要等紅綠燈走行人穿越道時，您可曾注意到號誌燈裡有那些或走或跑的小綠人嗎？你可知道行人號誌燈裡的小綠人或小紅人是誰設計的嗎？答案是德國人。在 1961 年時，一位名叫 Karl Peglau（1927-2009）的德國心理學家，將當時單色的號誌燈改成一個人形樣貌的號誌，當時蔚為創舉。

2000 年時，靜態的人形標誌演變成跑步的動畫。而動態的小綠人及小紅人上面，還有一個裝置是倒數的秒數，這個點子是由臺灣人想出來的。在 1999 年，臺北市政

Pedestrian signals with countdown time

府的交通局，在信義區的松智路及松壽路的十字路口，設置了全世界第一個有倒數讀秒的紅綠燈，讓用路的行人有更明確的指示，能充分掌握過街時間。這個設計不但被廣泛地運用在全國各地的行人穿越道及車道上，並很快地就得到世界各國的賞識，到目前為止，美國、德國、日本、中國皆採用了這個道路交通號誌的設計，小綠人與小紅人從此便在每個街口為用路人做導引小天使，守護每位用路人的路權。

3.5 The Story behind the Little Green Man Traffic Sign

As long as you have the experience of walking across a street in any major city worldwide, chances are that there would be a little green man shown at the traffic light guiding the pedestrians through the crosswalk. If you see the little green man start to run, you'd better pick up your pace to make your way through.

Traffic lights for pedestrians used to have just the solid colors in green and red, signaling "good to go" and "stop," respectively. In 1961, a traffic psychologist, Karl Peglau (1927-2009), in what was then East Berlin of East Germany, turned the solid-color signs into silhouettes of a man in the striding motion or at a standstill. At the time, the "walking green man" and the "standing red man" were only static signs, instead of animated ones, and remained so for many years.

According to the Department of Transportation of the Taipei City Government, the world-famous "little green man" animated traffic light was born on March 18, 1999, at the intersection of Songzhi Road and Songshou Road, Taipei, Taiwan. Based on Germany's previous model, the newer version added a countdown timer and animated motions. The countdown timer would indicate to pedestrians how much remaining time there is for

Pedestrian traffic lights

the crossing. The animated signals, shown as a green man walking or running, or a red man standing still, further reinforce the traffic messages to pedestrians. The countdown timer is particularly helpful for those pedestrians who need sufficient time to cross or for those who can easily cross within the last few seconds.

This newer model of traffic signal has brought Taiwan into the spotlight of international attention. Not only have Taipei City and the rest of Taiwan fully implemented this traffic device, but countries such as the U.S., Germany, Japan, and China have also been impressed by the design and decided to adopt it. The little green man now serves as a guardian for pedestrian safety in many parts of the world, thanks to some thoughtful industrial designers from Germany and Taiwan.

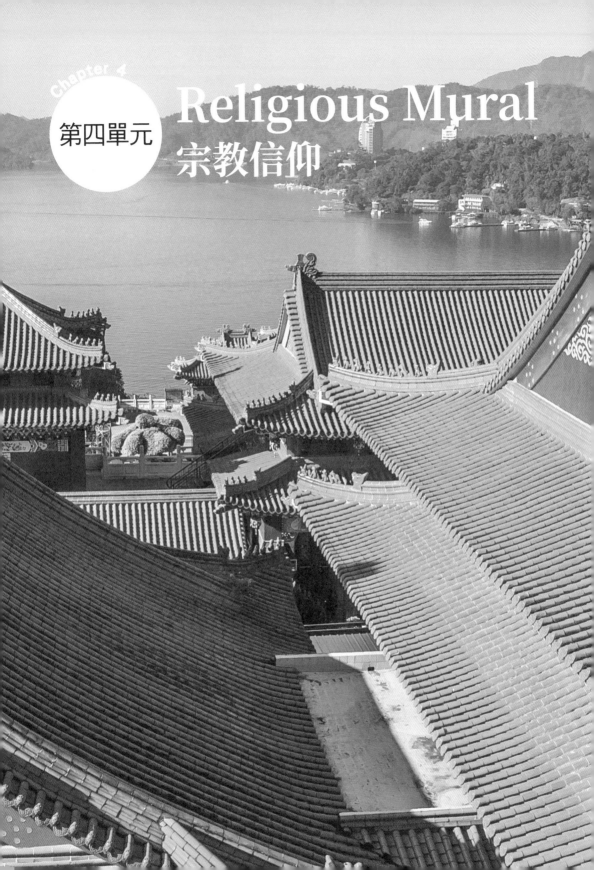

Chapter 4

第四單元

Religious Mural
宗教信仰

4.1 宗教多元

　　根據一項調查，臺灣的宗教包容度在全世界 232 個國家中名列第二，僅次於新加坡，該調查報導不同的八種宗教信仰在世界各國中出現的比例，其中，臺灣人民近半數的宗教認同是民間信仰，第二高的信仰為佔五分之一人口比例的佛教，百分之五為基督教，約十分之一人口的臺灣人沒有任何宗教信仰。

　　民間信仰可謂五花八門，從祖先祭拜、神靈祭拜、到靈物靈獸祭拜等皆有可聞。臺灣四處廟宇林立，供奉的神祇也大有不同，佛教、道教、淨土宗等不同的教派也有不同的戒律與信念，相較於世界的各大宗教派別，臺灣的小眾民間信仰更為普遍，走在大街小巷中，隨處可見廟宇林立，人民的信仰多元，無神論者更是大有人在。臺灣人民的宗教信仰不是家族傳承，也不是與生俱來，而是個人選擇的呈現，與西方世界中各大宗教的信仰方式，可謂大相逕庭。

Taipei Truth Lutheran Church

4.1 Religious Diversity

● ●

According to a report released by the Pew Research Center, a U.S.-based nonpartisan fact tank that informs the public about trends shaping the world, Taiwan ranked second among 232 countries and territories in the Religious Diversity Index (RDI) in 2014, second only to Singapore. On a scale of 0 to 10, Taiwan scored 8.2 while Singapore scored 9. A total of eight religious classifications, including Buddhist, Christian, Folk Religion, Hindu, Jewish, Muslim, Other Religion, and Unaffiliated, are listed in the study. Based on the percentage of a nation's population belonging to the eight major religious groups, the study reports how close a country has equal shares of the eight religious orientations (Taiwan Today, 2014).

The highest percentage of the eight religious practices in Taiwan comes from Folk Religion, which represents 44.2 percent, followed by Buddhism at 21.3 percent, Other Religions at 16.2 percent, and Christianity at 5.5 percent. Another 13 percent of the people surveyed are nonreligious (Liu, 2014). Folk Religion refers to shamanism, animism, and ancestor worship. Shamanism is the belief that the spirit world is accessible by some gifted practitioners. Animism is the belief that objects, places, and non-human creatures all possess spiritual power. Finally, ancestor worship is the belief that the deceased could still wield influence over the living (Quarterly, 2016).

The various forms of folk religion observed in Taiwan may date back to Taiwan's history and immigrant culture. While the Communist Party suppressed folk religion after taking over China in 1949, folk religion thrived under the Kuomintang's (KMT) ruling in Taiwan. Walking down any street in big cities such as Taipei or small townships such as Beigang, one will find Taoist temples next to modern churches or mosques. Early immigrants from Mainland China and recent immigrants from Southeast Asia, as well as the aboriginal communities, have brought with them a spectrum of religions to settle into their new home. Instead of a clear divide between secular and religious zones, people have woven their worship practices into daily life.

The religious landscape in Taiwan has reached a new height. In light of the religious intolerance and ideological conflicts worldwide, Taiwan's religious diversity is an example of how freedom of expression and religious tolerance can bring about cultural enrichment and spiritual blossoms (Peng, 2016).

Taipei Grand Mosque

Holy Family Church Taipei

Grace Baptist Church

Lungshan Temple in Taipei

4.2 廟宇文化

　　臺灣目前有超過一萬二千多所的廟宇（台灣宗教巡禮，2017），在大街小巷中崢嶸並存。因為宗教的多元，以及民間信仰的百花齊放，臺灣的各個寺廟滿足了香客及遊客探訪的不同目的，香客到他們信奉的廟宇祭拜神明，為親友祈福，也尋求心靈上的慰藉；遊客到各個寺廟參觀，除了欣賞廟宇本身的建築與藝術之美，也能觀察到平民百姓日常生活的脈動。廟宇在臺灣不僅僅是宗教的活動場域，更是人民展現活力的地方。

4.2 Temples and Rituals

Countless temples dot the landscape across Taiwan, from magnificent palaces to small shrines. The huge ones are multi-layered, sending worshippers and visitors wandering from one interconnected chamber to another; the small ones are no bigger than a highway toll booth tucked aside a major intersection in a city. Contingent on the gods and goddesses worshipped in the temples, many temples are built and decorated differently. In general, the Buddhist temples are usually less ornate than the Taoist ones, which involve more folk religious practices and carry more folk deities. However, if the temples are historically significant such as the Lungshan Temple (established in 1647) in Lukang, central Taiwan, the carved pillars and walls inside the temples are usually mesmerizingly full of delicate details, regardless of their Buddhist or Taoist origins.

Each temple usually houses more than one deity unless it is a tiny shrine. In enormous temples such as Lukang Lungshan Temple (鹿 港 龍 山 寺) or Beigang Chaotien Temple (北 港 朝 天 宮), the main chamber would house Guan Yin – the goddess of mercy, compassion, kindness, and love. Guanyin (觀世音), translated as listening to all of humanity's cries, began her divine existence in India as the male bodhisattva Avalokiteshvara, but is usually portrayed in Taiwan as the Buddhist goddess of mercy. Another deity commonly worshipped in prominent temples is The Jade Emperor (玉皇大帝), often regarded as the creator of the universe. Mazu (媽祖), the sea goddess, is a mortal-turned-deity figure worshipped in over 850 temples in

Taiwan. Also co-existing in other altars under the same roof of a temple are: the fertility goddess, Zhusheng Niangniang (註生娘娘), to whom women pray for conceiving a baby, The Old Man under the Moon (月下老人), to whom people pray for finding their destined soulmates, and The City God, Chenghuang (城隍爺), to whom people pray for justice and safety because he protects cities and manages all the affairs of

Inner gate in Lungshan Temple Taipei

the underworld. Still, there is another human-turned-deity god, GuanGong (關公), who was a fierce general during the Eastern Han Dynasty. He is worshipped for his loyalty and courage, often as a door god at the temple's main gates to ward off evil spirits. Finally, the Earth God (土地公) might be the deity who often stands alone in a small shrine in different corners of a city guarding people's wealth and fortune. As there may be up to 36,000 gods and goddesses in the Taiwanese pantheon, it is nearly impossible to list all of them here.

As for the façade of a temple, some common features are present. First, the temple's roof is usually decorated with deities and mythological creatures

Fertility goddess altar at Lungshan Temple

Xingtian Temple in Taipei

that signify good luck and ward off evils, much like the gargoyles on the rooftop of churches in the West. Second, towering stone pillars with delicate carvings of dragons, phoenixes, or other lucky animals are hallmarks of a well-built temple. Third, a pair of stone lions usually appear at the front of the temple. They may look identical, but a closer look will reveal that the one on the left is a male lion holding a coin or a ball. The one on the right is female and has a baby cub under her chest. These stone lions serve as the guardians of the temple. Fourth, larger temples typically have three entrances. The central entrance is reserved for gods and not meant to be used by worshippers. When facing the temple, the right entranceway is for worshippers to enter; the left doorway for people to exit, thereby creating a counter-clockwise traffic path. Doors are painted with Door Gods to ward off evil spirits. Finally, at the bottom of each gate sits a vertically raised wooden sill meant to be stepped OVER, not on. Door sills provide worshippers and visitors a chance to acknowledge their entry into the sacred home of gods. Evil spirits are said to be incapable of making the move and therefore barred from entering the temple.

Inside a temple, there is usually a wall full of glowing lights, known as Guangmingdeng (光明燈), or bright blessing lights. These lights are actually a myriad of tiny light bulbs, each inside a small glass box engraved into the wall. Each glass box also sits a miniature effigy of a deity worshipped in the temple. All the blessing lights are dedicated to those who have made donations to the temple in the previous year. Each year, around the Lunar New Year, people would pay a visit to their favorite temple and donate to have a blessing light lit in a box. These blessing lights are meant to guide their way through potential obstacles in the coming year. Many families would make donations to have each of their family members protected by a deity with a blessing light.

People visit temples not only to worship gods, often they want to commune with gods and seek advice. But how do gods deliver their messages? In Taiwan and many Chinese communities, a pair of crescent-shaped red wooden blocks, each with one flat and one curved side, known as jiǎo bēi (筊杯), are used to perform the ritual. When worshippers have a question seeking gods' advice, they will pray in front of the altar, silently saying their name, date of birth, residing address, and a yes-no question. Then they would toss the red moon blocks onto the nearby floor. How the two blocks land indicates the deity's answer to the question. Since it is a yes-no question, the answer would be "yes," "no," or "no comment." Two curved sides up indicate the gods' negative response to the inquiry. Two flat sides

Red wooden blocks

up mean the deity is laughing at the question's irrelevance or having no comment on the request. It takes one flat side and one curved side up to imply approval from the deity. If the appeal concerns significant life events such as marriage or funeral arrangements, a total of three positive tossings are needed to conclude the request. The seeker will be advised to drop the request if tossing the moon blocks consistently does not present positive results.

Walking into any temple in Taiwan, big or small, visitors would notice an incense burner in front of an altar. Worshippers would light up incense sticks, prepared by themselves or purchased at the temple, hold the incense stick while praying to the deities. Upon finishing their prayers, they would stick the lit incense into the incense burner, put their palms together and bow to end the prayer. More than often, joss paper, known as the monetary paper for the dead (冥紙), will be burned if the seeker's prayer is for their deceased family's well-being. The whirling smoke from the burning of the incense and joss paper is said to carry each seeker's prayer to reach the deities high up in the sky.

Temples in Taiwan serve as religious venues and community centers where people gather to socialize while celebrating important events. It is not unusual to see local elders playing chess or card games in the temples. Temples provide a comforting place for worshippers' spiritual seeking as well as their social needs. Regardless of one's religious practices, all temples welcome believers or non-believers to visit the sacred homes of deities.

4.3 媽祖遶境

媽祖是臺灣民間供奉的神祇，相傳是真有其人，在西元960年間，出生在中國福建省的湄州島，本姓「林」，因出生時沒有啼哭，而取名「默娘」，即「林默娘」。默娘自幼年即聰慧貼心，在她28歲時，因為營救父親與哥哥而溺死海中，她的勇敢讓她得以去凡升格為神祇。每當漁民出海遇到大風浪或海難時，相傳都曾見過默娘顯靈，世代之後，媽祖的名號便逐漸流傳開來。

西元1730年，中國福建省的一戶人家，遷居到臺灣，並將媽祖迎來臺灣，自此媽祖的名聲就更為遠播。為了紀念林默娘的生日，每

Mazu statue (Courtesy of David Yu)

年農曆3月23日，為期九天八夜的媽祖出巡就會在全國展開。起點是臺中大甲鎮瀾宮，由信眾扛轎迎媽祖出宮，途經各縣市的重要廟宇，所到之處萬人空巷，信眾會跪地膜拜，祈求媽祖保佑，虔誠者會平躺地上，讓神轎在身上通過，希望獲得媽祖最大的庇護。

九天八夜的出巡遶境，徒步約340公里，途經21個鄉鎮縣市、上百間廟宇，最後再迎回鎮瀾宮。這項每年的宗教盛事，已在2009年被聯合國教科文組織列為世界重要的文化遺產。

4.3 Mazu Pilgrimage

According to local legends, Mazu, a marine goddess, was said to be a real person born into a fisherman's family in 960 CE on Meizhou Island, Fujian Province in China. Surnamed Lin, MoNiang ("girl of silence") barely cried as a baby, thereby earning her the name "quiet girl." She was smart, sensible, and fond of learning. More importantly, she was able to communicate with the deities. MoNiang drowned at the age of 28 while trying to rescue her father and brother caught in a storm when fishing. The local fishermen immortalized her as a deity to honor her courage and altruism. Legends dictate that she often made her presence for fishermen caught in shipwrecks at sea. People began worshipping her as a mother figure of mercy. Generations after generations, people look up to Mazu (媽祖 "ancestor of motherhood") as the Goddess of the Sea who watches over them.

In 1730, Mazu migrated to Taiwan by a family in Fujian Province who worshipped the deity. Mazu has since become one of the most prominent gods on the island, with over 870 temples dedicated to her worship. Every spring, the 9-day Mazu Pilgrimage will start on the 23rd day of the 3rd lunar month to commemorate MoNiang's birthday. During the pilgrimage route, Mazu's statue will be carried in her palanquin by pilgrims and travel through major temples in several cities in Taiwan. Along the route, hundreds of thousands of worshippers will line up to welcome the arrival of Mazu. Many would kneel when welcoming the passing of the Mazu's palanquin. Some would bend down to allow the passing of the palanquin over their bodies, a

Mazu pilgrims (Courtesy of David Yu)

Mazu pilgrimage (Courtesy of David Yu)

Mazu's palanquin (Courtesy of David Yu)

Passing of the Mazu palanquin for blessings
(Courtesy of the Tourism Bureau in Taiwan)

pious action believed to bring blessings. Still, some would insist on walking through the entire trip of 340 kilometers, despite blisters on their feet. During the procession, festive activities will be held, including puppetry theatre performances, float parades, dragon and lion dances, and martial arts performances. The highlight of the procession occurs when Mazu returns, on the 9th day, to the Zhenlan Temple in Dajia, Taichung, where the largest celebration of all will take place.

Today, the pilgrimage stops at nearly a hundred temples across twenty-one townships throughout Taichung City and three other Counties, covering 340 kilometers in length and drawing over one million visitors each year. Dajia Mazu Pilgrimage has been named one of the top three religious festivals globally by the Discovery Channel (Wu, 2018).

Statue of the sea god, Mazu

In 2009, the beliefs and customs of Mazu were inscribed by the United Nations Educational, Scientific and Cultural Organization (UNESCO) as the intangible cultural heritage of humanity (UNESCO, 2009).

4.4 發光發熱的傳教士

臺灣最早在 17 世紀中期開始接受西教的傳入，當時佔領南臺灣的荷蘭人藉此傳播基督教，佔領北臺灣的西班牙人則傳播天主教，從西元 1624 年到 1662 年近 40 年的西方殖民期，基督教逐漸在臺灣萌芽。

1858 年，清朝與俄國、美國、英國、法國簽訂天津條約，規定臺灣開港准許傳教士自由進入傳教及建造禮拜堂。次年，道明會指派郭德剛神父（Fernando Sainz）來臺傳教，並於高雄地區建立臺灣近代第一座天主教堂。隨後郭德剛神父還在現今屏東縣萬巒鄉，建立了著名的萬金聖母聖殿，這也是目前臺灣所留存最早的天主教堂。

19 世紀末，醫學博士馬雅各（Dr. James L. Maxwell，1836-1921）正式受英國蘇格蘭長老教會海外宣道會所派，來到臺灣，開始真正具有深厚影響力的傳教工作。1865 年，馬雅各博士在現今臺南市開始設教行醫，他當時所設立的禮拜堂，即是現在太平境馬雅各紀念教會的前身。他的免費行醫之舉，初期卻受到民間的質疑與詆毀，說他偷死人器官配藥施醫，民眾向他丟石頭，官府下令院所歇業。馬雅各只好轉移到現今旗津地區，繼續傳教。經過數年的努力，馬雅各神父已能說一口流利的福佬話，信眾也日益增多，他的傳教奠定了長老教會在南臺灣的基礎。他的診所就是現今在臺南的新樓醫院。馬雅各神父的小兒子，後來也回到臺灣行醫傳教，謂為美談。

在馬雅各之後，又有巴克禮（Rev. Dr. Thomas Barclay）及馬偕（George Mackay）傳教士來到臺灣傳教。巴克禮神父為臺灣奉獻了一甲子的人生，籌辦設立了全臺第一所大學（府城大學；今臺南神學院）及第一份報紙（臺灣府城教會報）。另外，巴克禮神父與馬雅各神父皆致力於將聖經轉譯成羅馬拼音的臺灣話，為日後本土版聖經的推廣立下汗馬功勞。

1872 年，加拿大長老教會的馬偕（George Mackay）傳教士來到北臺灣淡水。和馬雅各神父一樣，馬偕經常受到排外的對待。曾經有民眾拿大刀欲砍殺他、教會被拆毀、座車被縱火，但馬偕從不害怕與退避，反而以鎮定與溫柔的態度讓大家信服。由於他全心的奉獻，漸漸地贏得老百姓對他的信任與尊重。馬偕在臺灣的 30 年間，協助設立了超過 60 間教堂，並創辦多所學校及後來的馬偕醫院，他最後選擇在臺灣終老，並在臺灣安息回歸天家。

從 17 世紀到現在，因為許許多多西方傳教士來臺，默默地為臺灣貢獻他們的一生，臺灣的醫療、教育及文化發展因此得以提升，他們當初因為傳教而離開家鄉，卻在臺灣找到另一故鄉，因為他們無私的貢獻，臺灣才有今日的風貌。

George Mackay

4.4 Missionaries

Throughout history, there have been missionaries who traveled thousands of miles to Taiwan to introduce Christianity to Taiwan's inhabitants. As early as 1629, Robertus Junius, a Dutch missionary, was sent to Taiwan by the Dutch Reformed Church (Anderson, 1998). During his stay from 1629 to 1644, he converted more than 6,000 Taiwanese indigenous people to Christianity. Like all the missionaries, Junius believed in bringing technology and Western medicine to non-Western countries to make socioeconomic change.

In 1859, Fr. Fernando Sáinz came to Kaohsiung, Taiwan, and established the Holy Rosary Cathedral (Minor Basilica) – the first Catholic Church in Taiwan. Christianity started taking root in Taiwan since then. In 1865, James Laidlaw Maxwell (馬雅各醫師), a Scottish doctor, arrived and opened a clinic in what is now Tainan. At first, the residents did not appreciate his kind act of free medical practice with free medicine and even accused him of stealing organs from his patients. His clinic was stoned and vandalized to the point that Dr. Maxwell had to move his clinic to Kaohsiung, where he continued to offer free medical

Resting place of George Mackay in Tamsui

services, especially his care for leprosy sufferers. Over time, people began to appreciate his kindness. As more locals came to his clinic as well as his Sunday services, Tai-Peng-Keng Church (太 平 境 教 會), also known as Maxwell Memorial Church, was founded as the very first Protestant church in Taiwan.

Maxwell's clinic, the first Western clinic in Taiwan, went through much expansion over the centuries and has now become a beautiful hospital, still called Sin-Lau Hospital (新樓醫院). Maxwell's two sons, having followed their father's footsteps, also became physicians and missionaries. One of the sons, Dr. James Maxwell Jr., returned to Taiwan to practice medicine at Sin-Lau Hospital from 1900 to 1923. He was warmly welcomed and beloved by the locals.

Another remarkable contribution by Maxwell was his work on creating a localized Bible. By working with biblical scholars, linguists, and other fellow missionaries, he helped complete the revision of the Taiwanese Bible in 1933, which has been used by the Presbyterian Church in Taiwan ever since.

Born in Scotland, Reverend Thomas Barclay was among the longest serviced missionary (1875-1935) in Taiwan. He came to Taiwan at the age of 26 and devoted the rest of his life to Taiwan until he passed away in Tainan at the age of 86. Throughout the 60 years of his missionary work, Barclay's dedication to Taiwan was above and beyond. He established the Tainan College (府城大學), now called Tainan Theological Seminary, the very first college in Taiwan at the time. In 1885, he started the first newspaper, Taiwan

Hu-Sia Church News (臺灣府城教會報), now called The Taiwan Church Press (臺灣教會公報). Moreover, he helped translate the original version of the Bible into Romanized Taiwanese, which allowed him to introduce the gospel to the people of Taiwan. Essentially, he helped modernize the missionary work in Taiwan.

The first Presbyterian missionary to Taiwan was George Leslie Mackay, who the Canadian Presbyterian Church commissioned to go to Taiwan in 1872. At the age of 28, Mackay arrived in southern Taiwan and later settled in Tamshui in northern Taiwan, where he remained for nearly 30 years until passing away in 1901. Among Mackay's significant achievements and contributions to Taiwan was the establishment of Mackay Clinic in 1880, which was renamed, posthumously, the Mackay Memorial Hospital (馬偕醫院) in 1912 in honor of his lifetime devotion to the Taiwanese people.

Although Mackay was not trained as a physician, several foreign doctors assisted and accompanied him to treat patients who suffered from a range of tropical diseases, including malaria, which Mackay himself ended up contracting in 1873, one year after his arrival in Taiwan. He was able to overcome the difficulties and recovered. He was adamant in bringing the gospel to those who had not heard of Christ. Like many Western missionaries, Mackay was at first confronted by suspicion and hostility from the locals. People would greet him with stones, raw eggs, or human waste with which he would bear with patience. He also understood that the only way to reach the locals to spread God's message was to learn the local language, which he did within an amazingly short period of time.

Maxwell Memorial Church in Tainan

Through the help from local herding boys that he spent time with, Mackay was able to speak vernacular Taiwanese and reached out to more Taiwanese people, including the lowland aboriginals of the Kavalan tribe. Over time, people began to listen to his preaching and accepted his spiritual guidance. Throughout his lifetime in Taiwan, he helped establish over 60 churches and baptized more than 4000 locals, many of whom were of Kavalan ancestry.

In addition to his evangelization with the Taiwanese people, Mackay was best known for his dedication to establishing the Oxford College, now Aletheia University (真 理 大 學), Tamsui Girls' School (淡 水 女 學 堂) – the first school for women in Taiwan – and Tamsui Middle School, now Tamkang Senior High School (淡 江 中 學). In the school's eastern corner, there is a small cemetery where Mackay is buried. He made Taiwan his final resting place. He wrote in his book "From Far Formosa: The Island, Its People and Missions" in 1896 (Mackay, 2011), an ethnography and memoir of his missionary work in Taiwan:

"How dear is Formosa to my heart! On that island the best of my years have been spent. How dear is Formosa to my heart! A lifetime of joy is centered here. I love to look up to its lofty peaks, down into its yawning chasms, and away out on its surging seas. How willing I am to gaze upon these forever! My heart's ties to Taiwan cannot be severed! To that island I devote my life. My heart's ties to Taiwan cannot be severed! There I find my joy. I should like to find a final resting place within sound of its surf, and under the shade of its waving bamboo." – My Final Resting Place (Kellenberger, 2016)

"Better to burn out than rust away" (寧願燒盡，不願腐銹) is Mackay's motto, much like a glimpse of his lifetime contributions to Taiwan. In addition to these historical figures, there is still a myriad of missionaries in different parts of Taiwan right now, devoting the best years of their lives to build and sustain a better education and health care system in Taiwan.

Chapter 5

第五單元

Holidays &
Festivals
節慶與祭典

5.1 重要節慶

....

農曆新年

　　農曆新年、端午節、中秋節並列為臺灣的三大節慶。農曆新年傳統上是家人團聚的重要節慶，與西方的聖誕節相似。每年農曆新年大概會落在西曆的一月或二月間，傳統上會慶祝整整 15 天，從除夕夜到元宵節（年初十五）都算是新年的期間。

　　農曆新年的起源已不可考，相傳最早在中國商朝時，人民為了祭祖會在年初或年末舉辦慶典活動。到了周朝時，有了「年獸」和「歲」的概念，讓人們開始使用紅色的器物來趨吉避凶，從此紅色便代表了吉祥的顏色，是過年期間的代表色。紅包的象徵意義與使用，據稱也在此時開始，未成年的孩子，在除夕夜守歲到午夜，為家中的長輩添壽，守歲守到越晚，長輩就會越長壽，也是流傳下來的習俗之一。

端午節

　　端午節是在每年的農曆五月五日，節氣上屬溽暑的開始，代表萬物將蓬勃旺盛的生長。

　　端午節的由來是相傳在中國的戰國時代，屈原（公元前 340 年～公元前 278 年）是輔佐楚國君王的丞相，也是一位憂國憂民的詩人，他擔心君王受讒言所困而苦心建言，但最後仍不得君王信任，而被放逐到深山裡。

　　因為楚國的日漸衰敗，被當時的秦國打敗並佔領，屈原悲痛絕望，自盡於汨羅江中。人民一心想將他的屍骨打撈上岸，因而划船四處尋找，端午節划龍舟的傳統便是由此而來；在遍尋不著屈原的屍骨後，人民又想到用竹葉包裹米飯，丟入汨羅江中餵食魚蝦，讓魚蝦們不去啃食屈原的身體，爾後這個作法逐漸演變成端午節包粽子的傳統。

Chinese New Year snacks

中秋節

　　中秋節的由來，相傳最早是在周朝時，皇帝會在秋季月圓時分供禮祭拜，為下個豐收的季節祈福。到了唐朝，王公貴族會在秋天滿月時分，以賞月之名，飲酒笙歌聚會。隨後到了宋朝，便直接將農曆的八月十五日，明訂為中秋節。

　　中秋節是家人團聚的重要節日，若是家人好友在異地無法團聚，也會特別引人思念，一如蘇軾的詞：「但願人長久，千里共嬋娟」，即便相隔千里，但看著皎潔的月亮，知道在世界的另一端也有同樣仰望月亮的家人與朋友，藉著溫柔的月光聯繫了彼此，而不再感到孤單失落。

　　中秋節的應景食物就是圓圓的月餅，傳統的口味有豆沙、棗泥、蓮蓉等，近年來業者推陳出新，陸續推出創新口味如抹茶、榴槤、或冰淇淋口味的月餅。不管月餅的口味如何變化，能在明亮無暇的月光下，與家人團聚，品茶談心，才是中秋節最重要的意涵。近年來，每逢中秋節，家家戶戶還會以戶外烤肉的方式來過節，蔚為流行。

5.1 Major Holidays

Chinese New Year

Chinese New Year is a two-week celebration, starting on the 30th of the twelfth lunar month – New Year's Eve – and lasting until the 15th of the first lunar month – Lantern Festival. During the two-week period, people reunite with families, return to their hometowns, or visit temples. Businesses and government offices are usually closed for the holidays on New Year's Eve and won't reopen until the 5th of the first lunar month where people would resume work. Shop owners would light firecrackers outside their shops to draw commotion. More importantly, the loud noise of firecrackers is believed to be able to drive away bad luck and signify the beginning of another promising year for the businesses. On the 15th of the first lunar month comes the Lantern Festival in which people carry lanterns of all shapes and sizes on the streets or go to see huge lanterns on display at parades. Lantern Festival presents the highlight of the celebrations and marks the end of the New Year's period.

The exact origin of the Chinese New Year is not documented. Some believe that it originated in the Shang Dynasty (1600 ~ 1046 BCE), where people held ceremonies in honor of gods and ancestry at the beginning or the end of each year. In the Zhou Dynasty (1046 ~ 256 BCE), the term "Nian" – year – was established in folktales. People believed Nian to be a mythical beast that ate animals, crops, or humans on the eve of a new year. However, they later found Nian feared the color red and loud noises. To prevent Nian from attacking the villagers, people would set off firecrackers and decorate their households in red. This practice led to the custom of lighting firecrackers on New Year's Eve and hanging red lanterns or red scrolls at doors or windows.

Aside from monster Nian, another mythical demon called "Sui" (age) is related to the practice of giving red envelopes to children or unmarried youth. Legend has it that Sui would come out to terrify children at their bedsides on New Year's Eve. Children who had been scared by the demon would develop a high fever and become hysterical. As such, parents would light candles and keep vigil for their children. On one New Year's Eve, the parents in one household gave their child eight coins to play with during the observance. The youngster wrapped the eight coins in red paper, which was incidentally placed under his parents' pillow after falling asleep. As demon Sui came to touch the child on the head, he was protected by the intense glow radiated from the eight coins, which turned out to be eight fairies. Since then, giving red envelopes ("yāsuìqián" 壓 歲 錢) – suppressing Sui money

Chinese New Year's Eve dinner

– has become a tradition during Chinese New Year, symbolizing the care for children and the desire for good luck. The practice of midnight vigil on New Year's Eve has also become a custom. Some even believe that the more vigilant children are on New Year's Eve, the more longevity it would bring to the elderly in the family.

Dragon Boat Festival

Dragon Boat Festival is one of the major holidays observed in Taiwan. The holiday falls on the fifth day of the fifth lunar month each year. It's a holiday that commemorates and honors the life and death of a patriotic poet, Qu Yuan (qū yuán 屈原) (340 ~ 278 BCE), who lived during the Warring States Period (475 ~ 221 BCE) in ancient China. Qu Yuan served as the top advisor to the king in the State of Chu. His dedication earned him the king's trust. The king, however, was misled by other officials who were accusing Qu Yuan of treason due to jealousy of the king's favoritism to him. As a result, Qu Yuan was sent into exile.

Zòngzi, sticky rice wrapped in bamboo leaves

Dragon boat racing

The powerful State of Qin later conquered the State of Chu while he was in exile. Feeling powerless to save his beloved country, Qu Yuan committed suicide by drowning himself in the Miluo River on the fifth day of the fifth lunar month. Upon learning of his death, the local people were deeply saddened because he had been a respected State Advisor prior to his exile. Efforts were made to rescue his body in the river only to receive no results. Out of desperate measure, cooked rice wrapped in bamboo leaves was dropped into the river to feed the fish that would otherwise feed on Qu Yuan's body. They also deployed boats to search for Qu Yuan's whereabouts. Boat rowing eventually turned into dragon boat racing, whereas lumps of sticky rice in bamboo leaves evolved into the current "zòngzi" (粽 子) – a signature food eaten during the holiday celebration. Although "zòngzi" is often called "rice dumpling," it is far from any kind of flour-based dumplings.

Mid-Autumn Festival

Mid-Autumn Festival, also known as the Moon Festival, is one of the most popular events and falls on the 15th day of the eighth lunar month every year. The origin of the Moon Festival may be traced back to the Zhou Dynasty (1045 ~ 221 BCE), during which Chinese emperors would worship the harvest moon in autumn, believing that it would bring them bountiful harvests the following year. Moongazing became popular during the Tang Dynasty (618 ~ 907 CE) among wealthy merchants and court officials who held glamourous parties in their courtyards, drinking and dancing while appreciating the bright moon. During the Song Dynasty (960 ~ 1279 CE), the 15th day of the 8th lunar month was designated as the Mid-Autumn Festival.

A variety of moon cakes

Mooncakes are, without a doubt, the most significant pastry for the Moon Festival. Traditional flavors include red bean paste, lotus seed paste, date paste, and pineapple paste. In recent years, bakeries have introduced novelty flavors such as green tea, durian, or chocolate. No matter how the flavor or the filling may change, mooncakes remain a tangible symbol to unite all family members under the same bright moon. In recent years, people have enjoyed celebrating Moon Festival with outdoor barbeque parties, turning it into a National Barbeque Day.

5.2 鬼月

　　每年的農曆七月是臺灣俗稱的鬼月，七月初一是地獄鬼門大開的時候，猛鬼出籠，生人迴避。因為陽間充滿了陰間來的鬼魂，所以須萬事小心，避免到溪邊、海邊玩耍，以免被溺死的鬼魅抓交替；窗邊或床邊不要懸掛風鈴，才不會無端招來遊走的鬼魂，種種禁忌都出自因敬畏鬼魂所衍生的告誡。

　　農曆七月十五日則是中元節，這天全國各地的寺廟都會舉辦盛大的中元祭典，擺出豐盛的祭品，來慰勞陰界來的各路好漢，尤其是沒有後代子嗣祭拜的亡靈，特別容易在陰界感到貧乏困頓，中元普渡的精神就是希望能對所有的亡者給予安慰與祭拜，即便不是家人，也都一視同仁。這樣恩澤廣被的精神源自於目連救母的故事：目連是釋迦摩尼的弟子，有神通力可以觀到法界，他知道他已去世的母親在冥界很飢餓，就想提供她食物，但不管是什麼食物，只要母親一拿到嘴邊，就變成熊熊烈焰灼燒她，根本無法進食。目連很難過，就向釋迦摩尼請示，釋迦摩尼說，你必須恭敬地邀請眾多虔誠的和尚，為母親念誦超渡，才能化解她在陽間所做的諸多惡業。目連很誠心地照做了，結果因為許多和尚的祝頌，不但順利超渡了自己的母親，也解救了很多其他在餓鬼道的亡靈。自此以後，這樣的典範便流傳下來，為了不認識的亡靈，也能很虔誠的祭拜與助念，希望他們都能早日抵達彼岸極樂世界，這就是普渡的由來。

　　在鬼月要結束時，會舉行「搶孤」及「跳鍾馗」的儀式，將還在陽間停留的鬼魂招喚回冥界，以關地府之門。鬼月的各種儀式與習俗，都源自於臺灣人對鬼神的敬畏，而中元普渡的精神則是對所有的亡靈都給予慰藉，希望能藉此減少他們的受苦與折磨，也是基於對所有眾生的愛護。

Ghost Festival offerings

5.2 Ghost Month

During the seventh lunar month of the year, people in Taiwan observe Ghost Month as a cultural event. People believe that the gate to Hell would open on the first day of the seventh lunar month. Ghosts wandering in the underworld would roam the Earth when they enter the living world. When the spirits return to the underworld on the last day of the month, the gate would once again be closed.

As the living world can be filled with spirits who venture in from Hell during the entirety of Ghost Month, people are warned against a variety of taboos that can cause misfortune. For example, do not go to any unattended rivers or beaches. During the Ghost Month, chances are high that more drowning cases may occur as wandering souls would look for human bodies to possess to be reborn. It is not recommended to blow whistles at night as they attract spirits to follow people home. Unless absolutely necessary, avoid remote mountain areas or abandoned houses where spirits tend to gather. Do not hang dry laundry at night as spirits are said to hide inside the wet clothes and affect the minds of those who put on the clothes later. Taoist priests use bells to summon spirits, especially those who die in an accident; the wind chimes tinkling can incidentally attract unwanted souls, thus hanging wind chimes by the windows or bedsides should be avoided. It is also during Ghost Month in which weddings, buying a car, or moving into a house are to be averted.

The 15th day of the seventh lunar month, halfway into Ghost Month, is the month's highlight called Chung Yuan Festival (中元節). The origin of Chung Yuan Festival dates back to the Han Dynasty around the 1st century where people worshiped their ancestors and showed empathy to the wandering spirits. While Chung Yuan Festival is a common practice in Chinese culture, Ghost Month is only practiced in Taiwan and Singapore.

During Chung Yuan Festival, in many notable temples in Taiwan, altars are laden with various offerings to fete the ravenous spirits who die without offspring. The purpose of the festival is to offer deliverance to the deceased families and strangers as well. People believe that those who die without offspring would be doomed to suffer from starvation in the underworld.

The annual offerings during the Chung Yuan Festival allow hungry ghosts a temporary release from hunger.

The idea of offering oblations to deceased strangers traces back to a Buddhist story "Maudgalyayana rescues his mother." Maudgalyayana is the Sanskrit version of Mulian (mùlián 目連) in Mandarin. Mulian was a dedicated disciple of Sakymuni (釋迦摩尼), which is Sanskrit for Buddha. One day during his meditation, he had a vision of his deceased mother in the form of a hungry ghost craving for food. He was strongly saddened by the fact that his mother had been starving in Hell, and used his power to bring food to her. However, as soon as the food reached his mother's mouth, it turned into flames. Mulian was deeply troubled by his inability to save his mother from suffering. After consulting with Sakymuni, he realized that his mother had been greedy and unkind to many people when she was alive. Because of these sins, she was punished after death and forced to turn into a hungry ghost who would suffer from endless starvation. Her past sins were too weighty for Mulian to lift alone.

Sakymuni told Mulian that the only way to free his mother from eternal hunger was to collect prayers from as many monks as he could possibly gather. On the 15th day of the seventh month, Mulian offered fresh fruits and a hearty meal to those monks who came to chant for his mother. The collective incantation worked to release Mulian's mother and many other hungry ghosts who were suffering in the realm. Mulian's initial intention was to save his mother, but due to the group chants' collective piety and fervor, the kindness reached above and beyond his own family into those deceased strangers. People believe that a powerful liberation will be

Joss paper or ghost money

bestowed upon the departed spirits only if the living perform virtuous deeds.

Therefore, the Chung Yuan Festival's essence lies in the act of universal salvation for all suffering beings. Ceremonies are performed to honor both the deceased ancestors and strangers. In Taiwan, the traditional offerings generally include three types of meat (chicken, pork, and fish 三牲) and four types of fruit (四果), with fruit offerings presented only in odd numbers. Moreover, certain fruits, such as bananas, plums, pears, and pineapples, cannot appear on the altar tables together because they mean "come to my house" when pronounced in Taiwanese, which could attract the wandering spirits the wrong way.

When food could be scarce in bygone times, offerings at great abundance were meant to show people's sincerity towards their ancestors and other spirits. Nowadays, it is becoming more and more popular to offer vegetarian oblations during grand-scale ceremonies.

Throughout Ghost Month, many ceremonial activities are performed, including the release of water lanterns and Chiang Ku (qiǎng gū 搶孤). The releasing of water lanterns takes place on the 14th night of Ghost Month. Paper lanterns in the shape of a house or a lotus flower are lit and released into a river or ocean. The lit water lanterns are meant to provide comfort and illuminate the way to the afterlife, especially for those spirits who have drowned. The donors of the water lanterns will write various blessings on the lanterns. The farther the lanterns float, the greater blessing the donors will receive. It is believed that a departed spirit following a water lantern has reached ashore when the candle in the lantern extinguishes.

Chiang Ku, translated as "vying for offerings to fete the loner souls," is an event performed at the end of Ghost Month. It is a contest in which a high-rise tower made of bamboo poles is erected for contestants to scale, at times as high as 143 meters. On top of the tower are sacrificial offerings in honor of the spirits without descendants. Whoever can reach the top of the bamboo tower the fastest to fetch the target sacrifices wins the contest. As the bamboo poles are covered with grease which makes the upward climb extremely difficult, contestants must be skillful in completing the climb without falling. Winners are awarded with sumptuous prizes and will be blessed for the upcoming year. The pounding of drums and cheering crowds fill the event and are meant to drive away those wandering ghosts reluctant to leave the living world.

The final ritual of the month is "Dancing Chong Kuei." Chong Kuei (zhōng kuí 鍾馗) is a legendary god known for his power to expel demons. By performing the Chong Kuei dance on the last day of Ghost Month, lingering ghosts who haven't returned to the underworld are summoned and captured by the ritual. Every year, the Lao Da Gong Temple (老大公廟) in Keelung hosts the ceremonial opening and closing of the gate to Hell, a tradition that has persisted for more than 160 years.

Ghost Month in Taiwan is an annual event practiced by all walks of life. Although the event's fundamentals are based on Buddhism's universal salvation and Taoism's redemption of souls, it is hardly a religious event. People observe the event simply due to their respect and awe for the deceased families and strangers.

5.3 王船祭

　　每三年一次，在十月或十一月舉行的「王船祭」，是臺灣西南沿海地區很重要的廟會活動之一。燒王船的典故是送瘟神出境，早期由福建渡海來臺的先民，因為醫療環境不佳，傳染病的橫行造成人民恐慌，因而藉由祭典的舉行，祈求神明護佑。如今臺灣醫療發達，人民已不再因疾病而惶惶不可終日，燒王船的祭典也演變成祈安降福的活動。

　　屏東東港的王船祭是臺灣最大的王船祭典，東港人所造的王船是仿效古代戰船，施工費時，雕工精美，彩繪細緻，精美程度堪稱全臺之冠，東港因此有「王船故鄉」的美譽。三年一次的燒王船祭典，醮期共七天，第一天「迎王駕」是到鎮海里海邊邀請王爺自地府駕臨人間；「過神火」由乩童過火顯靈。第二天開始的連續四天是「王駕出巡」，王爺坐鎮的王船會繞境東港鎮各區及鄰近鄉鎮，以收瘟疫邪靈。第六天是王船「陸上行舟」繞境法會，由廟會的祭司誦經，將王船引領至海邊；第七天清晨破曉時分「送王」，在成千上萬民眾的目送下，美麗莊嚴的王船，載著瘟神王爺以及無數被降伏的疫鬼邪靈，一起在大火中前往靈界，讓人民未來三年免於災厄邪靈的干擾。

Glamourous King Boat (Courtesy of the Tourism Bureau in Taiwan)

Demons aboard! (Courtesy of David Yu)

5.3 Boat Burning Festival

Every three years in October or November, a seven-day ceremony begins in Donggang, Pingtung County in southern Taiwan. The Burning of the King Boat (燒 王 船) , a ceremony to pray for peace and tranquility, is a popular event and the one in Donggang is the biggest in Taiwan. On the first day, thousands of people would gather on a beach to watch the rituals of inviting the plague-control gods back to Earth. These gods, known as Wang Yeh (wáng ye 王爺) or Royal lords, are Taoist deities responsible for curing illness and plague. Legend holds that during the reign of the Tang Dynasty's

King Boat parade (Courtesy of David Yu)

Emperor Taizong (626 ~ 649 CE), 36 high-ranking officials and scholars drowned from a shipwreck incident (Crook, 2018). Emperor Taizong deified them as protective spirits capable of preventing calamities. Descendants later referred to these protective spirits as Wang Yeh, an honorary title to glorify their bravery for fighting epidemic and plague demons.

During the seven-day ceremony, devotees perform divination rites and liturgies to invite the plague gods to help expel the demons. Spirit mediums who are psychics would walk on fire without being burnt or hurt when possessed by the plague deities. Having welcomed the Wang Yeh back to Earth, the ceremony will proceed to traditional lion dancing, stilt walking, and martial arts. Over the next few days, a massive King Boat parade carrying palanquins of Wang Yeh would go across town, capturing all remaining demons in the living world. With all the spells and chants from Wang Yeh via spirit mediums, people believe that the plague demons would become entrapped within the King Boat.

Once the parade is complete, followers would fill the boat with offerings and stacks of joss paper, along with the statues of Wang Yeh aboard. Each King Boat is beautifully decorated with paintings of dragons and flowers. The 2012 King Boat cost NT$7 million to build, thanks to all the volunteer craftsmen who were firm believers of the protective Wang Yeh. On the last day of the ceremony, the burning of the King Boat signifies the highlight of the event. Deep into the night between 10 pm and 11 pm, Taoist priests would again chant spells and perform rituals to summon all demons to stay aboard the boat.

Burning of the King Boat (Courtesy of David Yu)

Burning of
the King Boat
(Courtesy of
David Yu)

Glamourous offerings of food, as many as 108 dishes, would be prepared to honor Wang Yeh for their hard work of protecting the living world from disease and illness. Around midnight, the Boat would be put on wheels and hauled to the beach, accompanied by exploding fireworks. On the beach lie piles and piles of joss paper around the King Boat to help fire ignition. It is not until 5 am would the King Boat be engulfed by fire, allowing Wang Yeh to usher all the plague demons back to the underworld, thereby dispelling misfortune and bringing tranquility for the next three years.

The Boat Burning Festival was brought to Taiwan by immigrants from China in the 18th century. At the time, diseases or epidemics could easily wipe out the lives of the villagers. In fact, malaria was only brought under control as late as 1965 in Taiwan. Having little scientific or medical assistance, early settlers resorted to folk religious practices that helped them find ways to manage their struggles. Now that Taiwan is no longer a pestilential place, the folk religious festival has evolved into a symbolic ceremony praying for peace, stability, and welfare for the living people while honoring the deified martyrs.

5.4 原住民祭典

　　臺灣目前有 16 個原住民族，他們的部落分布在臺灣的各個地方。這些南島語系的族各自有自己的族語，還有對他們意義重大的各種祭典，在每年的不同時節裡舉行。這些祭典充滿了對大自然的崇敬、對祖先的感懷、以及對族人的相互照顧。最著名的祭典有阿美族的豐年祭、排灣族的五年祭、泰雅族的播種祭、布農族的打耳祭、太魯閣族的感恩祭、卑南族的猴祭、魯凱族的黑米祭、鄒族的戰祭、賽夏族的矮靈祭、達悟的飛魚祭、噶瑪蘭族的海祭、邵族的拜鰻祭、撒奇萊雅族的火神祭、拉阿魯哇族的聖貝祭等。

Amis Harvest Festival (Courtesy of the Tourism Bureau in Taiwan)

5.4 Aboriginal Festivals

Among the 16 officially recognized aboriginal tribes in Taiwan (Charette, 2020), Amis (阿美族) is the largest, with over 210,000 members. Amis Harvest Festival (豐年祭) is one of the major events celebrated by forty Amis communities in Hualien and Taitung, eastern Taiwan. These communities hold the festival separately in their native villages to celebrate the millet harvest from July through August. The length of each festival ranges from one day to seven days, pending different villages. Amis people rely on millet, a grain similar to rice, as a staple crop. Millet can also be ground into flour or brewed into millet wine. During the harvest season, Amis people show gratitude to the bountiful season while honoring their ancestors' spirits for blessings and protection. It is also a homecoming celebration for family reunions and bequeathal of traditional culture to the younger tribal members.

The festival is partitioned into three phases: welcoming the spirits, feasting with the spirits, and sending the spirits off. Usually, the young males of the tribe would be in charge of welcoming the ancestral spirits whereas female members of the tribe would be sending the spirits off. During the ceremony, Amis people dance and sing in a circle holding hands and stepping in sync with one another. Singing and dancing symbolize their gratitude for a bountiful harvest. Amis people believe that the joy they experience in singing and dancing this life will impact their afterlife. The Harvest Festival gives them an opportunity to pay tribute to their ancestors, share joy with their tribal members, and pray for another fruitful year. It is also during the festival that young members of the tribe would openly search for their marriage partner in special rituals.

From March to June every year, the Tao tribe (達 悟 族) who resides in Orchid Island of Taitung, southeast of Taiwan, will celebrate the Flying Fish Festival (飛 魚 祭). It is the only oceanic tribe among the 16 tribes, with a population of 4300 members. Flying fish, or "Alibangbang" in the Tao language, are their primary food source. Beginning in March, the Kuroshio Current brings shoals of flying fish to the waters near Orchid Island. Because the Tao people consider flying fish a gift from heaven, fishing season is seen as a sacred ceremony. Many rules and restrictions apply. For example, women and tourists should not touch the fishing boats without permission as it will bring bad luck to the fishermen. Oranges, considered a curse, should not be present near beaches or harbors during the fishing season.

The special fishing boats, the "tatara" for 1~2 people and the "chinurikuran" for 8~10 people, are made of 21 or 27 planks of wood and painted with beautiful totemic patterns in black-white-red traditional Tao colors. Black means "dignity;" red represents "passion," and white symbolizes "ocean waves." Each boat is a piece of art. The totems include human figures, waves, and a sun image meant to ward off evil spirits. Before a new boat is placed into the water, there will be a launching ceremony where the Tao people in traditional outfits lift the boat into the air multiple times to pray for their ancestors' blessings.

The festival comes with a series of rituals, including the blessing of the boats, praying for a plentiful catch, summoning the fish, first-fishing-

Flying Fish Festival (Courtesy of the Tourism Bureau in Taiwan)

night ceremony, fish-storing ceremony, and finally, the fishing cessation ceremony. During the rituals, men wearing the traditional Tao loincloths and silver helmets would sing and dance to pay their utmost respect to the gift from heaven.

Fishing boats of Tao people in Orchid Island, Taitung

Some species of flying fish, specifically black flying fish, are only reserved for the elderly members of the tribe. Those who mistakenly eat the wrong flying fish would likely become ill. After the fishing season ends, there are traditional ways to preserve the annual catch. Tao people would soak the fish in seawater first before hanging the fish to dry under the sun. It is taboo, especially for visitors, to trespass people's lawns where flying fish are being sun-dried.

Another tribal festival, The Holy Shell Festival (聖貝祭), comes from the smallest tribe, Hla' alua tribe (拉阿魯哇族), which has a population of 400 members in inland Kaohsiung, southern Taiwan. The Holy Shell Festival, Miatungusu in Hla' alua language, is a ritual worshiping the shell gods in charge of different aspects of life for Hla' alua people. A shell, Takiaru, was considered a sacred treasure by their ancestors. The festival, held every two or three years for six days after the crop harvest, is the biggest among all rituals in the tribe.

Each shell (Takiaru) represents a god. Currently, there are twelve Takiarus: (1) Pavaasu (Bravery) to empower people as warriors; (2) Paumala Papa'a (Hunting) to help people hunt animals; (3) Pamahlatura (Health) to keep people healthy; (4) Paumala Aanu (Food) to bring people abundant food; (5) Hlalangu 'Ihlicu (Exorcism) to ward off evil spirits; (6) Patama'iiaru (Diligence) to encourage people to work hard; (7) Pamavahlauvau (Peace) to bring tranquility to people; (8) Kupamasavau (Sloth Exorcism) to drive laziness away; (9) Paumala Ngahla (Optimum) to bring people success; (10) Pamaiatuhluhlu (Protection) to keep people from harm; (11) Papacucupungu (Intelligence) to bring people intelligence; and (12) Sipakinivaratuhlausahlu (Wind and Rainfall) to bring favorable weather and keep natural disasters away. Since Takiaru collectively governs many aspects of people's lives, it has become the almighty entity worshipped by the Hla' alua people and the totem of the tribe.

Each of the 16 recognized aboriginal tribes in Taiwan has its own significant festivals held throughout the year. These festivals are the culmination of their respect and awe for their ancestry and deities, and celebrate their vibrant cultures and customs.

Chapter 6

第六單元

Culinary Delights
飲食文化

6.1 鼎泰豐

因為歷經日據時期,以及 1949 年大陸各省級人士隨國民政府遷臺的影響,臺灣的飲食可謂包羅萬象,大江南北的食物在大街小巷的餐廳幾乎隨處可見,這些多元的飲食特色也讓臺灣的餐飲更添風貌。

鼎泰豐是臺灣第一家獲米其林一星級的餐廳,在 1958 年以油行起家,但後來賣油的生意表現逐年下滑,而轉型賣小籠包,沒想到漸漸做出口碑。1993 年被紐約時報報導,名列全世界十大美食餐廳之一,從此聲名大噪。鼎泰豐最有名的品項就是小籠包,每一顆小籠包都有一定的黃金皮、餡比例,而且師傅皆在恆溫、恆濕的環境中完成擀皮、搓餡、包裹的動作,因為嚴格的品質管控,蒸好的小籠包,每個皮薄透明、肉汁豐盛,但卻不會輕易因筷子夾起而破餡,是最受歡迎的招牌料理。因為認真的經營態度,鼎泰豐目前已是臺灣在海外最有名的餐廳業者之一。

The original Din Tai Fung store

6.1 Gourmet Dumplings at Din Tai Fung

• •

Influenced by Japanese fare from its colonial past and the refugee chefs from China's different provinces, Taiwan's cuisine often defies boundaries and carries a rich mixture of tastes. It is very common to find food in Taiwan offering a plethora of cuisines such as Japanese sushi, Cantonese (廣東) dim sum, bold Sichuanese (四川) spices, or delicate Shanghainese (上海) dumplings, just to name a few. These delicacies made their way to Taiwan, either from colonization or immigration, have often localized with indigenous flavors and enriched Taiwan's culinary personality.

One of the first few Taiwanese restaurants recommended by the New York Times and the Michelin Guide is Din Tai Fung (鼎泰豐), famous for its premium dumplings (xiǎo lóng bāo 小籠包). First established as a cooking oil retailer in 1958, Din Tai Fung transformed into a restaurant in 1972 when the oil business declined. Steamed pork dumplings were among the house specialties. In 1993, Din Tai Fung made it into one of the top ten gourmet restaurants globally by the New York Times. It was also the only Taiwanese restaurant on the list. Since then, Din Tai Fung had been expanding its brand into many locations. More fame came when the Hong Kong branch was awarded one Michelin Star in 2010, the first of its kind for any Taiwanese restaurant. Now Din Tai Fung has restaurant locations in Australia, China, Dubai, Hong Kong, Indonesia, Japan, Macau, Malaysia, Philippines,

Singapore, South Korea, Thailand, the United Kingdom, and the United States.

In any location, there is usually a long line of people outside the restaurant. Some restaurants even go as far as to put out an LED sign with calling numbers to seat their customers. To ensure the quality of the world-famous dumplings, Din Tai Fung takes great pride in standardizing the making of each dumpling. In their masks and chef uniforms, all dumpling makers work in a temperature-controlled, moisture-controlled glass room, visible to the entire restaurant. This way, the dough would not dry out during the process. Each pork dumpling, a signature piece, should weigh 21 grams, with 5 grams of filling and 16 grams of dough. There should be precisely 18 folds on each dumpling. The number 18 has its significance. When pronounced individually in Mandarin, one (yāo) eight (bā) sounds like "yào fā," which means "getting rich." Each dumpling with 18 folds consumed by the customers would enhance the wish of getting rich once. Imagine the collective power of selling thousands of these dumplings a day in all locations across the globe!

Steamed dumplings are served in a bamboo basket steamer to retain heat and fragrance. There is a recommended procedure to appraise each dumpling. First, use chopsticks to pick up a dumpling by its top nubbin where the 18 folds come together. The skin of each dumpling would have become so thin, after being steamed thoroughly, that any poking could easily pop the filling out. And yet, the delicate skin would reliably hold a good amount of broth and meat when picked up by the top nubbin. Gently dip it in a mix of vinegar and soy sauce. Place the dumpling back into one's spoon. With a pinch of slivered ginger, which is meant to balance the filling's meaty flavor; one can bite a tiny hole to let the heat escape and suck the broth out as well. Suppose a dumpling is devoured in its entirety in one bite. In that case, one could risk popping the soup out of the mouth, like biting into a ripe tomato, and most importantly burning one's tongue because these dumplings are supposed to be served piping hot!

Din Tai Fung's steamed dumplings' success lies in its perfect combination of the paper-thin wrap and flavorful filling. Other competitors may have dumplings of the same look, but the wrap may be too chewy or its filling too heavy, rendering a disproportionate combination of the two crucial factors. Aside from the pork dumplings, there are also fish, shrimp, and vegetable dumplings. In recent years, new flavors such as pork-&-crab or pork-&-truffle dumplings have hit the menu and are well-received by patrons.

As for desserts, dumplings with sweet sesame paste or chocolate fillings

Long lines outside a Din Tai Fung

Busy chefs

may revolutionize people's impression of dumplings. When biting into a dumpling with the same 18 perfect folds, one may expect the meat's succulent broth. Instead, a creamy sesame paste or molten chocolate can flow through one's teeth with silky consistency, offering a sensational experience on the taste buds. Din Tai Fung has undoubtedly taken the making of dumplings to a whole new height.

Aside from dumplings, there are also many signature dishes, including Steamed Chicken Soup, Potsticker-style Gyoza, Shrimp-&-pork Wontons in Red Chili Oil, and Fried Rice. These delicacies all share the spirit of Shanghainese cuisine. Over the years, Din Tai Fung aims to keep flawless control of the food and services it provides by standardizing its recipes and staff training. Because of its global expansion of the business, multilingual menus are available in many locations around the world.

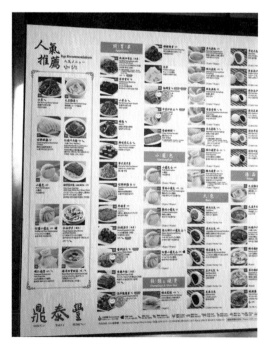

Din Tai Fung's multilingual menu

6.2 夜市文化

　　夜市是臺灣很獨特的文化，每個大城市裡都有不只一個夜市，它是當地人會去吃小吃、購物、聚會休閒的地方。許多夜市的形成來自人民群聚的地方，比如寺廟、醫院、或交通樞紐處，例如基隆廟口夜市、新竹城隍廟口夜市就是在廟宇附近形成的夜市；高雄的六合夜市則發跡於鄰近的醫療診所；臺北的華西街夜市因在碼頭附近，是自古商賈交會，人潮聚集而形成的夜市。

　　食物與商品是夜市的最大賣點，著名的臺灣小吃如蚵仔煎、臭豆腐、滷味皆是觀光客必試的品項。臺灣是水果王國，芒果、草莓雪花冰完全運用了新鮮的當地食材，為甜品帶來全新的體驗。另外，夜市裡會發現的商品小販，大至家庭用品，小至玩具服飾，無所不賣，議價更是購物的遊戲規則，若不想吃虧，需謹遵「貨比三家不吃虧」的原則。大型夜市如臺北的士林夜市，更有很多老少咸宜的娛樂設施。夜市為臺灣在地人提供了一個休閒的去處，也為觀光客提供了在地文化的嚐鮮處。

Shida Night Market

6.2 Night Markets

Night markets are one of the most distinguishing features that shape the nightlife in Taiwan. The areas covered by a night market may seem like any ordinary community. When dusk arrives, however, the neighborhood would suddenly come alive and turn into a massive party where street vendors pop out their stands with all kinds of goodies while people have to elbow through their way to move around. The hustle and bustle of a night market stay vibrant from dusk to midnight. When the rest of the city is calling it a day, a night market is just about to pick up its pace. Night markets provide not only food but also a venue to entertain all interests and all ages.

There are so many night markets in Taiwan that it is impossible to name them all. All major municipalities have a few night markets that thrive from urban development. In Taipei, Shilin Night Market (士林夜市), Ning Xia Night Market (寧夏夜市), Huaxi Street Night Market (華西街夜市), Raohe Street Night Market (饒河街夜市) are among the famous ones that attract many international tourists and locals alike. In Keelung, Miaokou Night Market (基隆廟口夜市) is always packed with crowds who are visiting a nearby temple. Another night market next to a temple is the Hsinchu City God Temple Night Market (新竹城隍廟口夜市). In Taichung, a city in central Taiwan, Fengjia Night Market is a popular hangout place for students from nearby universities. In Kaohsiung, a city in southern Taiwan, Liouhe Night Market (六合夜市) originated from the gathering of street vendors near a hospital in the 1950s and is now one of the most famous night markets in Taiwan.

Night market vendors   Street delicacies

The primary selling point of night markets is, of course, the food. There are all kinds of snacks and delicacies in night markets. Oyster omelets are a traditional Taiwanese snack made of eggs, oysters, corn starch paste, and vegetables. The sweet-spicy sauce accompanying the omelets will enhance the flavor of the snack. Stinky tofu is another signature snack for which Taiwan is famous. Visitors can not miss it when passing by a stinky tofu stand because of the strong smell. The tofu is made from fermented tofu brined in salt water; it can be steamed or deep-fried and often served with pickled vegetables. The strong scent of stinky tofu is very polarizing, especially for foreign visitors; people either hate it or love it, much like how they feel about durian.

Night market food in Taiwan

Another must-try snack in every night market is Salted Crispy Chicken or Taiwanese Popcorn Chicken (xián sū jī 鹹 酥 雞). These are bite-size chicken nuggets deep-fried, sprinkled with salt, pepper, and other spices. Although the main ingredient is chicken, various items such as seafood and vegetables are also available for one to mix and match. From among all the readily fried tidbits, each customer is free to pick their favorite ones, which will be deep-fried only briefly to resume optimal crispiness. Similarly, Stewed Food (lǔ wèi 滷 味) works in the same way, only that all items have been pre-simmered in a tasty herb-rich broth. Vendors selling stewed food often have an extensive display of food items, including braised chicken wings, chicken drumsticks, bean curds, seaweed stripes, noodles, and vegetables, just to name a few. Customers are to pick their favorite items which the vendor will warm up again and serve on a plate with seasonings of soy sauce and chili. Stewed food goes particularly well with beer and is a popular food choice for casual gatherings.

As for desserts, shaved ice covered with fresh fruit or toppings of various sweets is the most popular dessert during the hot summer months in Taiwan. The creamy texture of shaved ice offers a splendid eating experience. A bowl of shaved ice with diced mango topping is a mouth-watering dessert for many foreign visitors and locals alike. Strawberry and kiwi also make great toppings. Since Taiwan is famous as a Kingdom of Fruits, various fruit toppings offer an endless list of shaved ice combinations. Speaking of desserts, the chewy, sweet tapioca balls inside a cup of milk tea makes the drink more like a dessert than a beverage. Taiwan's signature drink is, without a doubt, bubble milk tea (see Chapter 6.3 for more details). Besides milk tea, customers can also choose from green tea, black tea, oolong tea, and fruit tea to mix with the tapioca balls. Finally, another liquid dessert is Hot Grass Jelly (shāo xiān cǎo 燒仙草) which is made from a mint-like herbal plant. When served hot, the grass jelly would melt into a gooey soup into which different toppings can be added; when served cold, the grass jelly can be gulped up through a straw to render a sensational drinking pleasure.

In addition to dazzling food options, people go to night markets in Taiwan for good bargains. Goods ranging from household appliances to clothing are available, and their prices are always negotiable. It is not uncommon to walk through a night market and come across very different prices for the exact same item. So, a rule of thumb is to always haggle for a better price and not rush into buying until a second or third offer is available. Street vendors even expect buyers to negotiate and believe that they have given in. Veteran night market goers often enjoy the negotiation process even if they can only cut down a few bucks.

Night markets in Taiwan offer people a venue for comfort food enjoyment, daily necessity purchases, and most importantly, entertainment for gatherings with friends and families. Locals rely on the vibrancy of the night markets while visitors feed on the wonders of night markets.

Mango shaved ice

Oyster omelet – a traditional Taiwanese snack

Fried stinky tofu with pickled vegetables

6.3 珍珠奶茶

　　珍珠奶茶是臺灣的國民飲料，它的起源據說是在 1988 年時，臺中知名的茶品店春水堂，有一位經理在開會時，無心地將手邊的奶茶摻入了臺灣特有的粉圓，粉圓的彈牙口感加上鮮奶與茶的滋味，帶來了前所未有的特別風味，粉圓加奶茶的組合因此一炮而紅。因為粉圓加入奶茶中後顏色變化有如黑珍珠，因而讓此飲品正式定名為珍珠奶茶。

　　隨著珍奶飲品在臺灣的大賣，也開拓了海外的商機，春水堂 2013 年在日本設店，隨後韓國、中國、美國、英國也都陸續有臺灣商家進駐設店，珍珠奶茶所到之處，皆蔚為風潮，所向披靡。更有趣的是，除了飲料，珍珠粉圓現在更搖身一變，作為更多其他料理的元素，比如珍珠蛋糕、珍珠鳳梨酥、珍珠口香糖、珍珠牡蠣煎等，看來珍珠粉圓的未來發展似乎無可限量，只等有心人去發掘了。

Bubble Tea

6.3 Bubble Tea

This signature drink is not any regular tea but milk tea, plus jumbo tapioca balls that swim and dance in the tea. These tapioca balls, known as "pearls" or "boba," are made from a mix of corn starch and brown sugar, thereby yielding an amber color for the balls after being thoroughly simmered in water. Simmering the bobas also makes them chewable. The chewy consistency is somewhere between jelly and the popular children's snack – "gummy bears." The chewable tapioca balls add a nice texture to the drink, especially when these balls come shooting up into one's mouth with a robust sip of the tea. Bubble tea is usually served in transparent cups to show its bubbly content against the creamy milk tea. It comes in a variety of flavors, like many teas, and can be mixed with fresh fruits and jelly. The

Bubble milk ice cream sandwich

Bubble milk snacks

extra ingredients often make it more of a snack than a drink as the starch-based balls can be very filling. It is no wonder that school youngsters are often seen grabbing a cup of bubble tea on their way home after school. It has become the equivalent of coffee for many adults as well. It is much like a non-alcoholic dessert drink that people of all ages fancy.

The sensation of bubble tea started in Taiwan in the 1980s, although there is no proven evidence about the origin of bubble tea. One story goes that during the 80s, teahouses or tea stands in Hong Kong and Taiwan were all vying for more market edge. A teahouse called Chun Shui Tang (春水堂) in Taichung, Taiwan, started serving Chinese tea cold – a technique the teahouse founder learned from his visit to Japan where coffee was served cold. In 1988, the teahouse's product development manager, Ms. Hsiu Hui Lin, was sitting in a staff meeting and drinking her iced tea. She had brought with her some traditional Taiwanese dessert, a sweetened tapioca pudding. Just out of spontaneity, she started mixing the tapioca balls into her Assam iced tea. This experimental beverage impressed everyone at the meeting. Once it got on the teahouse menu, it became an instant hit on the market and quickly outsold all the other items on the menu (Chang, 2017). The rest is history.

These days bubble tea shops appear on every corner of the streets in Taiwan. They've also ventured into neighboring countries such as Japan, South Korea, and China. Chun Shui Tang set up its first Japanese store in Tokyo in 2013. Soon afterward, a series of Taiwanese tea stores began to make their way into Japan. Interestingly enough, bubble tea has now evolved into novelty snacks such as bubble tea cookies and cakes. Who knows what the next invention out of bubble tea we might see on the market?

6.4 辦桌文化

　　華燈初上，你可曾在路邊看過臨時搭起的塑膠布帳幕，裡面有一桌一桌的宴席正在上菜中，菜色就像五星級飯店的酒席內容，有十幾道菜，每道都精心調配排盤，賓客有的衣著正式，有的則汗衫短褲，但都吃得津津有味，而布幕的另一邊則是備菜中的廚房，有的師傅正在切菜，有的正在烹煮，有的正在去魚鱗，而監督的大廚，人稱「總鋪師」，就是這些佳餚的幕後推手，這就是在臺灣大街小巷常見的辦桌文化。

　　辦桌文化緣起於日據時代之前，村民們藉由辦桌的宴席，來連絡情誼並擴展地方人脈，能夠承接大型的辦桌宴席的總鋪師，一定是經驗豐富的大廚，能夠設計出創意的菜餚，並在辦桌現場指揮若定，克服各種困難完成菜餚烹調、上菜，讓賓主盡歡，而時間一到，即收拾整理完畢，將現場恢復原狀，可謂是辦桌文化中的魔術師。

Setting up for a Bando

6.4 Bando – Roadside Banquets

Bando, a phrase in Taiwanese, means "to set or manage tables for dining." It is a practice often seen at weddings, birthday celebrations, religious events, or year-end company parties (wěi yá 尾牙). The number of tables can range from ten to thirty per event, and each table, usually a big round one, will seat ten to twelve people. The banqueting team consists of several cooks and assistants, headed by a master chef (zǒng pù shī 總鋪師) who designs the menu and supervises the serving of the dishes. For each bando event, there is usually an even number of tables and dishes, as even numbers are considered auspicious; unless the event is held as part of a funeral where an odd number of tables and dishes will appear. Ten or twelve courses of a meal are standard for a bando menu, and some menus can venture into sixteen or eighteen courses.

The sites to host a bando can be parking lots, community halls, school campuses, or simply secluding a stretch of road with tarpaulins and converting it into cooking and dining areas. The high mobility of bando dates back to the pre-colonial era before the Japanese rule. Communal feasts were a networking opportunity for locals and new arrivals to build connections. In rural areas where there were few restaurants to host communal gatherings, bando could take place anywhere and be up and go efficiently. By sponsoring a bando to treat their neighbors or even rivals, ambitious business people could strengthen their social ties and reputations.

In addition to the banqueting team, local helpers are often needed and recruited to help with the last-minute chores. For an evening bando, preparation usually starts in the early afternoon and goes well into the late night when the last pot is cleaned and stacked into the shipping truck. It is a time for the community to come together and reinforce social networks.

A bando host will usually request more than enough food for the guests to consume – a gesture to show one's generosity. Halfway through the meal, plastic bags will be put on each table for guests to pack unfinished food in each dish. Traditionally, fried food used to be a favorite item to pack because cooking oil was expensive for people to prepare deep-fried food at home during pre-colonial times. Most families only had boiled or steamed dishes. Bando occasions offered them a chance to indulge in crispy, fried food they barely had at home. Additionally, fried food tended to pack and travel well when people had to travel overnight or across townships to attend a bando event. Nowadays, Taiwan's thriving economy has seen less need for people to pack fried food home from a bando feast. The tradition of offering more than enough food than what guests can consume persists and, therefore, the custom of distributing bags for guests to bring food home remains.

In 2013, a comedy film titled *Zone Pro Site: The Moveable Feast* (總舖師), depicts how the daughter of a legendary bando master chef helps bring back the family glory. The film describes in great detail how a bando master chef should perform the following: cater to the exquisite needs of a sponsor, plan all the purchases and equipment, control the on-site workflow, respond to on-site emergencies in food preparation, supervise the cooking and serving of dishes, and finance the human and monetary capital. Rumor has it that

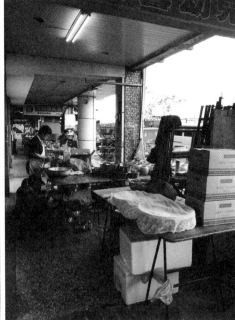

Along the sidewalks for a Bando   Bando caterers

one master bando chef once was catering a 245-table roadside banquet at a festival when torrential rains hit the site and tore down the tarpaulins. The stoves they brought to the site would not light, and some live shellfish they brought also escaped when the fish tank was overflowing with rainwater (Crook & Hung, 2018). It seems that bando feasts are fascinating due to their unpredictable nature and surprising "guests." Nevertheless, bando events are, without a doubt, a strong networking social event in Taiwan.

Chapter 7

第七單元

Social Pulse
社會脈動

7.1 性別友善

　　臺灣在 2019 年成為亞洲第一個認可同性婚姻的國家。這個里程碑代表了臺灣社會對同性族群與同性婚姻的接受度，在亞洲地區名列前茅。相較於歐洲國家早在 2001 年就已在法律上認可同性婚姻，臺灣的腳步雖然稍慢，但仍是世界上許多先驅國家之一。

　　早在 1986 年時，臺灣的立法院即有同性婚姻的提案討論，但當時的社會氛圍仍趨保守，未能成案。經過了 1990 年代的政治解嚴，在許多民間團體及社運人士的推動下，同性議題逐漸受到社會大眾的注意與關切。2016 年現任總統蔡英文贏得總統大選，她對同志人權的支持讓更多同性議題在臺灣百花齊放，經過許多草案的研擬與討論，終於在 2019 年 5 月 17 日在立法院通過同性婚姻的條款，讓法律上伴侶的結合延伸到同性族群。

　　歷經 33 年的社會變遷與時代脈動，臺灣在同志的人權伸張上又跨出一大步，為臺灣的人權歷史發展寫下另一頁美好章節！

Taiwan LGBT Pride 2019 (Courtesy of Taiwan Rainbow Civil Action Association)

7.1 Gender-friendly Country

On May 17, 2019, the Legislative Yuan in Taiwan passed the bill to allow same-sex marriage, making Taiwan the very first country in Asia to legalize same-sex marriage. As of October 2019, twenty-seven countries, mainly in Europe and South America, had recognized same-sex unions. In Europe, the Netherlands legalized same-sex marriage as early as 2001; Austria joined the band as recently as 2019. In the Americas, Canada was the first country to legalize gay marriage in 2005, followed by Argentina in 2010, the United States in 2015, and Ecuador in 2019. In the Pacific Rim, New Zealand and Australia are the only two countries that allow same-sex marriage (Felter and Renwick, 2020).

Although the legalization of same-sex marriage has put Taiwan at the forefront of its Asian counterparts, Taiwan has come a long way through an arduous journey. More than three decades ago, the Legislature in Taiwan first debated same-sex marriage in 1986. At the time, the society's heavy Confucian orientation did not have much maneuvering room for the LGBT movement. During the 1990s, Taiwan experienced a turmoil of political and social movements towards democratization. These reform efforts provided fertile ground for the gender rights movement. Taiwan's first gender rights organization, a lesbian organization called Between Us, was established in 1990. The first legally registered LGBT organization, *Taiwan Tongzhi Hotline Association*, was founded in 1998 (Chi, 2019). Along with various forms of LGBT artistic and cultural events, these civic groups helped lay out the fundamental groundwork for the same-sex marriage legalization to come into shape.

In 2003, then Vice-President and convener of the government's human rights commission, Annette Hsiu-lien Lu, drafted an article on same-sex marriage. This article, however, was only discussed among members of the cabinet. Two years later in 2005, then lawmaker Bi-khim Hsiao submitted a same-sex marriage bill to the Legislature only to be rejected. Despite legislative failure at multiple attempts, several public weddings for LGBT couples were performed, and Taipei still hosts an annual Pride Parade. In January 2016, presidential candidate Ing-wen Tsai won the election and became the country's first female president. Tsai supported same-sex marriage during her presidential campaign. Her electoral victory gave a significant boost to the LGBT campaigners.

Within a year after Tsai took office, more than 200,000 protesters showed up in front of the presidential building in Taipei, in December 2016, to demand a revision of the Family Law to include same-sex marriage, thereby triggering strong protests from various religious groups. The ruling Democratic Progressive Party (DPP) came under fire. After going through referendums, endless rounds of negotiations and confrontations among civic groups, the Legislative Yuan finally passed the bill and legalized same-sex marriage on May 17, 2019.

It has taken Taiwan 33 years to change people's mindsets towards gender rights. Against the backdrop of the Martial Law era (1949~1987) in which homosexuality was considered a big taboo, legalization of same-sex

Taiwan LGBT Pride 2018 (Courtesy of Taiwan Rainbow Civil Action Association)

marriage after three decades of hard work is truly a remarkable milestone in Taiwan's human rights history.

A gender friendly society

7.2 兩性平權在臺灣

　　臺灣在聯合國的兩性平權評比指數中，在 2017 年名列全球第八，在亞洲地區名列第一，遠勝於許多已開發的國家。在公職的兩性比例上，臺灣在 2016 年選出第一位女總統，擔任公職的女性比例遠高於英國與美國。在臺灣的工作職場上，女性參與工作的比例也高於日本、新加坡等國的女性；兩性薪資的差距也遠比歐美國家的小。

　　這些指標代表了兩性平權的社會進步，雖然臺灣在提供兩性平等的工作環境上，表現已居亞洲之首，但仍有許多進步的空間，期待未來有更大的進步。

Approaching gender equality

7.2 Gender Equality Conscious Taiwan

According to an annual report released by the Department of Gender Equality, Executive Yuan, R.O.C. (Taiwan) in 2019, Taiwan ranks 8th globally in the Gender Inequality Index (GII) and 1st in Asia based on data for 2017 (United Nations Development Programme, 2020). The GII is a composite index, developed by the United Nations Development Programme (UNDP) in 2010, that measures the inequality between males and females in 3 dimensions of health, empowerment, and participation in the labor market. A lower index value indicates a more gender-equal society. In the GII global ranking, Switzerland ranked 1st at 0.039, followed by Denmark at 0.040. Sweden and the Netherlands came in 3rd in a tie at 0.044. Compared to the 161 countries measured in 2017, Taiwan ranked 8th at 0.056, outperforming many developed countries such as Finland at 0.058, Iceland at 0.062, and Germany at 0.072. Compared with its Asian counterparts, Taiwan ranked 1st, outperforming South Korea, Singapore, Japan, and China, listed at 11th, 13th, 23rd, and 37th, respectively (Focus Taiwan, 2019).

Regarding the dimension of empowerment, the share of seats in parliament by women in Taiwan in 2017 was 38.1%, evidently outperforming UK at 28.5% and the U.S.A. at 19.7%. In 2016, Taiwan elected its first female president, Ing-wen Tsai, making it one of the few countries in the world with a female presidency. The proportion of women serving as local government heads grew from 6.3% in 2014 to 37.5% in 2018. This was also the first time in Taiwan's history that the female participation rate in government sectors exceeded one-third of the elected officials.

As for the labor force participation dimension, Taiwan's female labor participation rate, aged 15 and above, reached 50.9% in 2017, whereas the male participation rate was 67.1%. This labor force gender gap was lower than that in countries such as Singapore, Japan, and South Korea. On the other hand, Taiwan's gender wage gap had also declined from 18.2% in 2007 to 14% in 2017. Closing the wage gap means that women in Taiwan receive as much as 86% of the wage as their male counterparts. The observed gender wage gap is even higher in the U.S.A. (18.2%), Japan (31.9%), and South Korea (34.1%).

Over the past decade, Taiwan has made a lot of progress on gender equity advancement. There is hope that it will make even more significant strides on the Gender Inequality Index global ranking in the years to come!

7.3 臺灣的統一發票開獎

　　臺灣的企業型態主要是以中小型企業為主，財務的往來有很多是以現金方式完成，早期有很多企業逃漏稅的弊病衍生，有鑑於此，財政部在 1950 年代推出統一發票的政策，要求各企業在完成每一筆交易時，需主動開立發票，以便政府查核稅務。為了鼓勵民眾踴躍索取發票，特地開辦了統一發票開獎的行政配套措施，獎金從新臺幣 200 元到一千萬元不等，每二個月開獎一次，讓民眾承兌前二個月所有企業開立出的統一發票，只要有購物的發票，不限金額，也不限兌領人的國籍，只要發票號碼符合中獎號碼，即可在限定的時間內，到任何的便利商店兌領一千元以下小面額的獎金。自 108 年起，民眾更可以藉由手機下載軟體直接兌領儲存在雲端的發票（e-receipts），省去領取或蒐集紙本發票的煩惱。許多民眾常順手將發票捐出，讓公益或慈善團體接收以便兌獎，對於那些資金短缺、經營困難的公益或慈善團體來說，這筆每二個月的中獎金額，不論多少，都如天降甘霖，略有小補。財政部的這項創舉，可謂給政府及民眾帶來雙贏的效應，也是臺灣人民生活當中的小確幸。

7.3 Taiwan Receipt Lottery

If you are a fan of lotteries and regularly participate in lotteries, you must come to Taiwan to redeem some lotto prizes. In Taiwan, there is one lottery with free entry, the Taiwan Uniform Receipt Lottery. As the name implies, the lottery is based on every receipt you get from a purchase of any kind. The cost of the item does not matter either. The bi-monthly receipt lottery was introduced in the 1950s by the government to tackle tax evasion by some merchants. At the time, many businesses were not reporting their sales revenues as they should, thereby underreporting their taxes to the government. The Ministry of Finance decided to launch the lottery system that required establishments to issue a receipt for every transaction they completed. A majority of the businesses in Taiwan were, and still are, small- to medium-scale in size and handled transactions mostly in cash. This policy dictated that each transaction should be completed with a receipt given to the customer for every purchase, and a duplicate copy of the receipt would go to the Taxation Bureau. While the lottery system offers consumers an incentive to ask for a receipt and claim possible winnings afterward, it also helps the government track down businesses for taxation. In fact, this policy resulted in an immediate jump of the government's tax revenue by 75%. Having witnessed the win-win situation this policy allowed, the government gradually raised the maximum winning prize and most recently to the current jackpot prize at US$325,000 in 2011 for each cycle.

So how does the lottery system work? As long as you make a purchase, the merchant will issue a receipt, even for online purchases. The receipt is your golden ticket for the lottery entry. The eight-digit number at the top of each receipt will be the numerical code with which you claim your winnings. On the 25th

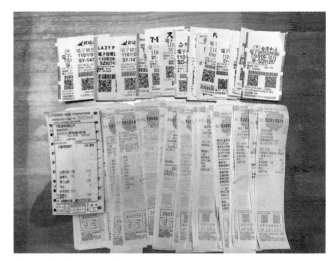

Taiwan Uniform Receipts

of every odd-numbered month, six sets of numbers will be randomly drawn in a televised event and announced on the Ministry of Finance website and major newspapers. The winning numbers are for those receipts issued in the previous two months. The total number of matching digits determines prize money. The jackpot prize of NT$10 million (US$325,000) requires a match of all eight numbers in the same order, whereas the smallest payout of NT$200 (US$6.50) only requires matching the last three digits in the same order as well. It is not unusual for people to win the jackpot with a purchase of the morning newspaper at NT$10 (US$0.33).

Many households would save all the receipts during the past two months and check against the winning numbers together. If the purchase is made via a value-added Easycard, an e-receipt can be stored electronically onto the card. These e-receipts will be automatically checked against the winning numbers as soon as the drawing occurs. The system will generate and send a text message to winners once their stored e-receipts have numbers that match the winning combinations.

The receipt lottery is open to everyone, including foreigners. Anyone with a winning number can take the receipt to redeem the prize money with a form of identification at a convenience store nearby. Larger winnings can be redeemed at banks. Many customers choose to donate their receipts right after a purchase by putting them into a box next to a convenience store's cashier because of the free entry fee. Boxes of receipts will then be given to charity groups to redeem any winning prizes. With a pile of receipts accumulated over two months, it's not unusual for a charity group to win extra thousands of dollars, made possible because of people's generous donations of their receipts.

If you are a traveler stopping by Taiwan next time, remember to hold on to your purchase receipts and check your luck two months later. Even if you are not in Taiwan when the winning numbers become available, you can still ask your friends to claim your winnings or donate your winning receipt to charity groups.

7.4 便利商店

　　臺灣的便利商店密集度高居世界第二，僅次於南韓，全臺目前有超過一萬家便利商店，每二千人就有一家便利商店。便利商店顧名思義，是提供簡便食物與生活必需品的商店，但臺灣的便利商店所提供的服務卻令很多外國人嘆為觀止。除了菸酒、食物、日常備品，還可以繳水電、信用卡、交通違規、稅務等各式帳單；訂購或領取交通旅行票券、藝術表演票券、運動競技票券皆可在店內自行操作完成。與各大便利商店合作的快遞業者也提供點到點的包裹運送服務，讓民眾選擇離自家最近的便利商店寄送或收取包裹，免除無人在家錯過包裹遞送或去郵局大排長龍的麻煩。各式各樣的熱食，讓晚歸或不開伙的人在深夜仍有熱食可吃。臺灣的便利商店文化為大都會緊張忙碌的生活方式提供了一個歇腳的地方，也為「便利」一詞賦予全新的意義。

A typical convenience store

7.4 The Almighty Convenience Stores

According to a Fair Trade Commission (FTC) report, Taiwan is ranked the second-highest globally for convenience stores' density per population (Focus Taiwan, 2020). For a country with 23 million people, there is a convenience store for every 2065 citizens on the island. Only South Korea boasts a higher number of convenience stores per population, one store per 1205 citizens.

Currently, 7-ELEVEN, FamilyMart, and Hi-Life are the three biggest convenience store operators in Taiwan, covering more than 75 percent of the stores and annual revenue. Like many other countries around the world, these convenience stores carry retailed goods such as food, beverages, tobacco and alcohol, stationery, and cosmetics. Nonetheless, the convenience stores in Taiwan have taken on much more functions over the years into their routine services.

People go to a convenience store to pay their bills such as utilities, traffic violation tickets, income and property taxes, etc. As long as the accounts are not past due, convenience store cashiers could simply scan the barcode on an invoice and process the payment. A stamp with a payment date on the invoice stub would serve as payment receipt.

All convenience stores in Taiwan operate like post offices. People send and

Goods at a convenience store

receive packages through a network of private couriers, separate from the postal service. These private couriers have door-to-door services, but they also ship packages from store to store, allowing customers an option to send and receive their goods in their nearest convenience store. Customers can pick up their online orders at a designated convenience store. This service is particularly friendly to those who do

ATM, ticketing kiosk, and photocopier in a convenience store

not have reception staff in their residence building and cannot be home at the time of delivery. Convenience stores could hold the goods up to a week for customers to pick up. Delivery service, however, is only limited to domestic destinations. International destinations still rely on regular postal service or other couriers.

Photocopy machines at a convenience store allow customers to scan, fax, print, and photocopy a document, making it a business processing center for those in haste. At a kiosk in the store, by inserting a flash drive or accessing an email or cloud account for the target file, customers can easily print out a hardcopy or obtain an image of the scanned file. Also accessible from those in-store kiosks, people purchase transportation tickets, concert tickets, sport events tickets, or add money to their individualized Metro cards. Even a pre-cooked 12-course Chinese New Year's feast is available on those kiosks to order!

Speaking of food, convenience stores in Taiwan have introduced all kinds of ready-made boxed meals over the years from which customers can choose. The choices range from Taiwanese cuisine (dumplings 包子 and porkchop rice 排骨飯) to Italian pasta and Japanese sushi. All meals have been pre-cooked and are ready for consumption once microwaved by the store staff following the precise heating instructions. These hot meals are essential provisions for those who work late-night shifts or are simply too busy to cook themselves. On a typhoon night when all the restaurants and grocery stores are closed, the 24-hour convenience stores with heartwarming meals could be a life-saving haven for those stranded by the typhoon.

There may be a fast-food establishment on every corner in major cities across the United States. In Taiwan, there may be more than one convenience store on every corner. First-time visitors to Taiwan may be in awe at the convenience stores' density. Still, they will soon experience the full capacity of the functions carried out by these stores. Because people dine and stop for coffee or snacks there, many convenience stores have turned the store decor into a cozy, homey style for their customers, attracting even more stable clientele. The 24-hour, 7-days a week store operation, providing services in food, drinks, transportation, and entertainment, has undoubtedly taken the "convenience" word to a new height.

7.5 垃圾不落地的 倒垃圾文化

●●

　　在地狹人稠的臺灣，尤其在大都市裡，大樓與公寓的住戶通常沒有多餘的空間置放大型的垃圾收集桶，亞熱帶的氣候也不允許垃圾堆積多日再予一併收集，有鑑於此，自 1997 年起，臺北市率先發起了「垃圾不落地」的政策，呼籲市民不要隨意棄置垃圾，而是將垃圾包好，在每日固定的時間，等垃圾車來臨時直接丟到垃圾車裡帶走，所有的垃圾都不再落地。這項政策剛執行時遭遇民眾抱怨，因為無法配合垃圾車來社區的時間，政府因而進一步調整垃圾車的路線與停留定點，讓民眾每日有多點多時的選擇可棄置家中的垃圾，因為這項政策的順利推動，臺灣從此脫離「垃圾島國」的臭名。

　　2000 年時，臺北市政府又推出「專用垃圾袋」的方案，規定市民只能用市府核准的垃圾袋來包裹、丟棄垃圾。因為垃圾袋須自購，而市民需購買及使用多少垃圾袋取決於自己製造的垃圾量，因此垃圾量得以大幅減低；且由於丟棄垃圾須使用自費垃圾袋，而資源回收則是免費的，因此這項政策同時也鼓勵了民眾積極回收資源。這項方案實施後，每日垃圾量即驟減 46%，民眾也因此認真的地做資源分類與回收，包括廚餘。熟食與生食的廚餘，經民眾分類後，再由環保大隊回收處理成豬飼料或堆肥，像這樣再次使用資源，而非像過去直接丟棄，已讓臺灣搖身一變成為全世界數一數二的環保國家，而民眾作為回收工作中重要的一環，那份大家一起參與的使命與責任感，讓政府的環保政策得以落實。

7.5 Trash Collection and Recycling

If you are from New Zealand, upon hearing the tune of Beethoven's Für Elise out on the streets, you may be out chasing an ice cream truck for your favorite sweets. But if you are in Taiwan, this world-famous music piece from Beethoven or "A Maiden's Prayer" from the Polish composer Tekla Bądarzewska-Baranowska simply means that it's time to take out your trash! (Paczek, 2017)

A classic yellow garbage truck

During the 1990s, Taiwan implemented a nationwide policy to "leave no garbage on the ground." This policy dictated that residents should take their trash out during specific timeslots at designated spots in their neighborhoods where garbage trucks would collect refuse and recycling. These garbage trucks are painted bright yellow with flashing lights to attract residents and to warn other motorists. It is the signature tune of "Maiden's Prayer" that reminds residents of the approaching garbage trucks. Rumor has it that Hsu Tse-chiu, the former head of the Department of Health, went with the classic tune in the early

A recycling truck

Multiple trucks on mission

Kitchen waste bin

1980s after hearing his daughter practice the song on her piano.

Before the enforcement of the policy, Taiwan was nicknamed "Garbage Island." People used to throw rubbish out on the streets at curbsides any time during the day. Garbage pile-ups soon attracted rats and cockroaches and often became public eyesores. Sanitary workers were simply overwhelmed to clean each site in a timely fashion. Unlike many countries,

Taiwan is densely populated and lacks adequate space for households to store rubbish before a truck comes weekly to collect the massive amount of trash. Furthermore, with the limited land area, the island was running out of space for landfill sites where toxic chemicals from decayed waste could leak into the soil and pollute the underground water. By the mid-1990s, two-thirds of the island's landfills were at or near full capacity. Garbage collection peaked in 1998 at 88.8 million tons. These alarming concerns had pushed the government to act fast to resolve the long-standing problem.

In 1997, Taipei launched the "Trash off the Ground" movement where trash was hand-delivered from households to garbage trucks without touching the ground. This movement, however, was met with some resistance at first. People complained that they couldn't comply with the trucks' schedule in their neighborhoods. The complaints were soon handled with more auxiliary measures and determination from the government. The city arranged garbage trucks' routes to allow multiple collection sites in a given neighborhood so that residents of the same area had more than one spot to bring their trash to every day. Some trucks came twice a day to a neighborhood; some would stay at a fixed point for a fixed period; some would come at this hour of the day and return four hours later across the street. These supportive measures were implemented to allow residents to toss their trash at a time and a spot convenient to them. Before long, everyone knows by heart when and where the garbage truck in their neighborhood would come. It has become a daily routine, just like grocery shopping after work or picking up kids after school.

In 2000, Taipei City took the initiative to begin the policy "Tax with the bag" or, in other words, a "bag tax." Residents have to purchase city-approved garbage disposal bags, which will internalize the waste collection taxes. This measure encourages residents to reduce waste and recycle. The amount of trash was immediately reduced by 46 percent, from 2497 tons to 1341 tons per day! Soon other cities and counties followed along and got on the bandwagon of Taiwan's waste management campaign. The "pay-as-you-waste" model encourages residents to seriously practice recycling and composting, both of which are free services. Plastic bottles, cans, and paper are to be sorted and recycled into a white truck that follows each yellow garbage truck.

Compared to New York City's "Recycle Everything" campaign, Taiwan's recycling campaign takes the practice to a whole new level. Residents are required to first sort their recyclables into different categories: plastic, aluminum/metal, glass, paper, and Styrofoam. Garbage trucks come five days a week and collect these recyclables on different days. If you come to the curbside with the wrong recyclables on the wrong day, sanitation workers that accompany each garbage truck will send you away without collecting them. No ifs, ands, or buts are accepted. As for kitchen waste, it is to be pre-sorted into two categories: cooked or raw. While cooked food waste will turn into food supplies for farm animals, raw foods such as fruit peels will become compost and fertilizers.

Today, Taiwan boasts a recycling rate of 55 percent, one of the world's top recyclers (Rossi, 2019). Its waste management plan implemented since the 80s has taken off. In addition to reducing the solid waste at landfill sites that could release harmful greenhouse gases and contaminants, the recycling industry now generates billions of dollars. Recycling companies can extract a high percentage of precious metals from consumer electronics – a genuine case of turning trash into treasure. Moreover, the kitchen waste that later turns into feed for animals or compost as fertilizers has created another window to an eco-friendly economy. According to the United Nations Environment Programme, one-third of all food produced worldwide, worth US$1 trillion, would go to waste. Richer countries, in particular, are more likely to contribute to food waste. If food waste could be reduced or reprocessed in more countries, it could help relieve the food shortage facing 795 million people globally who do not have enough food to eat.

As Taiwan tags closely behind the world's leading recycling nation, Germany, it has come a long way from the "Garbage Island" to a "waste-efficient" country (Rapid Transition Alliance, 2019). Residents have learned to be thoughtful and responsible for their consumptive behavior. The waste management plan, a pro-environment policy, has turned Taiwan's previous problem into one of its biggest assets.

Chapter 8

第八單元

Folk Practices
民間習俗

8.1 十二生肖

西方有依據出生月份決定一個人運勢的星象學，東方也有類似的概念，就是十二生肖。臺灣的十二生肖包含了鼠、牛、虎、兔、龍、蛇、馬、羊、猴、雞、狗、豬。這十二個動物生肖每年輪流擔任主角，每十二年就重新輪替。象徵尊貴的龍，是最受歡迎的一個生肖。龍年的嬰兒出生率一向很高，因為望子成龍的父母，都希望自己的孩子生來富貴，一輩子不愁吃穿，但諷刺的是，比起其他生肖的出生率，龍年出生的孩子卻因為更多同齡同儕的競爭，而面臨更多的挑戰與壓力。

至於十二生肖的由來有很多種說法，最常見的是玉皇大帝宣布，要在動物界舉辦一個渡河競賽，最先跑到終點的 12 種動物，才能進入「明星生肖排行榜」。每個動物都藉此大顯身手，最後由體積最小，卻最狡猾的老鼠奪得冠軍；好吃又動作慢的豬，則僥倖吊車尾上榜；本來很有希望名列前茅的貓，則被老鼠陷害，最後沒能入榜，遺憾之餘，也從此與老鼠誓不兩立。

Twelve Taiwanese zodiac signs

8.1 Taiwanese Zodiac

Much like horoscopes in the West, people in Taiwan and China use a 12-animal zodiac to determine a baby's sign, which could, in turn, predict a baby's personality traits. The twelve-animal zodiac consists of, in this order, Rat, Ox, Tiger, Rabbit, Dragon, Snake, Horse, Sheep, Monkey, Rooster, Dog, and Pig. As for how the twelve animals came to form the zodiac it is today, legend has it that it all started with a race announced by the Jade Emperor (玉皇大帝), the almighty King of the Universe.

Jade Emperor, being immortal, once asked an elderly man of his age. The elderly man replied, "I'm afraid I'm too old to remember my age." Jade Emperor thus said, "Perhaps we should use another system to count people's ages." The following morning, Jade Emperor summoned all the animals in his realm and said: "We will host a race tomorrow. Whoever arrives within the first twelve places will get to represent our zodiac." People only need to remember their sign as the birth year, thereby saving everyone the trouble of counting years for their age.

A massive number of animals in the forest would like to compete in the race. Some, such as the Rat and the Cat, were not as confident. They knew that part of the journey involved crossing a river that could easily drown them both. They needed to rely on another animal to ride across the river. They thought of their friend, Ox, who was a good swimmer. Cat and Rat then talked Ox into carrying them across the river.

Midway through the river, Rat, being a sneaky animal, pushed Cat into the river and urged Ox to keep moving forward. Ox, being naive, did not suspect much and moved on. While they were near the shore, Rat jumped ahead to reach the shore first. Rat won first place and became the first zodiac sign. Being a good-natured animal, Ox did not hold any grudges against Rat and was happy to claim second place in the zodiac, still ahead of many other animals.

After Ox, Tiger soon arrived, panting heavily as the river's swift currents almost washed it away. As a strong animal, Tiger was able to swim upstream and made it to the shore. The Jade Emperor named Tiger the third place in the zodiac. Following Tiger came Rabbit, who was hopping from stone to stone across the river. At some point, the water became so deep that Rabbit could barely hop and lost its balance. It grabbed unto a floating log in the nick of time, which later safely landed Rabbit ashore. Rabbit became the fourth zodiac.

Arriving in fifth place was Dragon. The Jade Emperor did not understand why a flying animal such as Dragon could take so long to arrive. Dragon then explained that it made a detour to help bring rain to the people in need. While getting back on track to the race, Dragon noticed Rabbit, soaking wet while clinging onto a log in the river. Being generous and kind, Dragon decided to help the poor Rabbit by sending a puff of its mighty breath to the log, thereby pushing it swiftly towards the shore. Feeling proud of Dragon's good deed, the Jade Emperor named it the fifth place in the zodiac.

As soon as Dragon reached the finish, Horse came galloping in full throttle. Little did Horse know that Snake had been hiding in the horse's hoof in order to hitch a free ride. Just before approaching the finish line, Snake jumped right out and startled Horse. Snake easily claimed 6th place, ahead of Horse, who had no choice but to take 7th place in the zodiac.

Not too far away came a squad of three animals, Sheep, Monkey, and Rooster. They had worked closely throughout the race. Rooster first spotted an old raft covered in weeds. Sheep and Monkey helped clean the raft and pulled it to the shore. Because of their joint efforts, the ride across the river was safe and smooth. The Jade Emperor was pleased with their good spirit and named Sheep the eighth creature, Monkey the ninth creature, and Rooster the tenth creature in the zodiac. Dog, arguably the best swimmer among all, came in only as the eleventh creature because it couldn't resist the temptation to play while in the water. Eleventh place did not seem to bother it at all.

Finally, the last animal to enter into the zodiac was Pig, who got hungry halfway through the race and had to stop for food. After gobbling down food and dozing off, Pig still made it back to the race and became the zodiac's 12th animal. While the Cat struggled to stay alive in the water, after the sneaky Rat forced it into the river, it finally made it to the shore. Unfortunately, Pig had already taken the last zodiac spot. Cat was too late to claim any standing. Because of Rat's vicious act in the race, cats and rats could never get along ever since.

During the year of the Dragon, birth rates in Taiwan will rise dramatically because people believe that babies born under the Dragon zodiac will be blessed with good fortune in their lives. On the other hand, certain zodiac signs, such as Rat and Snake, are not as popular as signs.

8.2 春聯

　　每逢農曆新年，家家戶戶都會在大掃除時，將門上舊的春聯拆下，換上新的春聯，為新的一年帶來新氣象。春聯在臺灣是過年時的慶典必備要件，春聯的源起早在明朝時期，人民為了避邪，在住家大門上掛起桃符，上有驅邪的門神畫像，以此阻擋邪靈進入家門，後來慢慢演變成在紅紙上寫出吉祥的話，貼在大門二側及上方，稱之為春聯的上聯、下聯、橫批。後來便成為傳統，每逢過年，家家戶戶都會貼上春聯，為家人及世界祈福。

Doorway spring couplets

　　春聯上的書法揮毫，讓春聯成為一項藝術創作，許多書法大家，每逢過年便會受人所託書寫春聯，他們或者將真跡致贈親友，或者印成現成的春聯供大眾購買。在臺灣，即便有名家揮毫的春聯可買，許多小學仍然會教孩子們書寫春聯，讓他們學會自己創作春聯的內容，並自己用毛筆完成春聯的書寫，使這項過年的傳統習俗能夠繼續傳承下去。

8.2 Lunar New Year Spring Couplets

Spring couplets, also called red scrolls, are a crucial part of tradition when celebrating the Lunar New Year in Taiwan. They are often seen at the front door of each household. Two vertical scrolls are pasted on the two sides of an entrance door, while a shorter, horizontal scroll is plastered above the door frame. Scrolls are always made of red paper on which wise words or poems in black or gold ink are written. There are also the diamond-shaped red scrolls on which only a single character inscribed. These diamond-shaped scrolls are placed right on the front door at eye-level.

On New Year's Eve, people will traditionally do their annual clean-up of the house in the hope of driving away bad habits and getting ready for a brand new year. New spring couplets will be prepared and posted at each house entrance, and old ones will be removed. Spring couplets are said to evolve from Taofu (táo fú 桃 符), a piece of peach wood board used in the Ming Dynasty during the 14th century. The peach panels were hung at the door with two guardian gods drawn on the panels to keep evils from entering the house. Calligraphers inscribed well-wishing verses on the peach boards to pray for peace. By the Qing Dynasty (1644-1911), spring couplets had become a form of art. These days, people write verses, instead of drawing protective gods, on red scrolls to pray for happiness and prosperity.

The two vertical red scrolls, pasted on two sides of a doorframe, are called the "upper line" (shàng lián 上 聯) and the "lower line" (xià lián 下 聯), with the upper line read first. The horizontal one, pasted across the top of the doorway, is called the "arc line" (héng pī 横 批). There is a trick in how to read these lines. Depending on the context, the Chinese characters can be read from right to left or vice versa. Readers often rely on their instincts to decide how to read a horizontal sign. If the arc line reads from left to right, then the left scroll should be read before the right scroll. If the arc line reads from right to left, the first line will then be the right scroll and the second line the left scroll. Fascinatingly, the arc line is always the last line of the verse. The arc line should cleverly summarize the entire passage. The couplets are also often rhymed and symmetric between the two vertical scrolls. For example, if the character "sky" appears in the upper line, there should be a mention of the character "earth" in the lower line. If the character "sun" shows up on the first scroll, expect to see the character "moon" on the second scroll.

Spring couplets are to be written by calligraphers who can write characters in their beautiful calligraphy strokes. In the old days, people used to bring blank red scrolls to famous calligraphers asking for their original, handwritten calligraphy. Nowadays, spring couplets pre-printed with famous calligraphers' works are available for purchase prior to the Lunar New Year. However, kids in school often learn how to write their own spring couplets and can bring home their own auspicious verses to hang on the doorways.

Finally, the square, diamond-shaped red scrolls, always written with one single character such as "happiness" or "Spring," are often pasted upside

Handwritten spring couplets for sale in a market

down on the door. Because "upside down" in Chinese, known as "dào" (倒), has the same pronunciation as the word "arrive" (到) in Chinese, an upside-down "happiness" red scroll infers that happiness would soon arrive. The same goes for "Spring would soon arrive" when the red scroll "Spring" is placed upside down.

8.3 送禮

　　贈禮在臺灣是很普遍的人情禮儀，舉凡婚喪喜慶，都需要包禮餽贈。通常婚禮會準備裝有現金的紅包，並在紅包袋面上寫吉祥話表示祝賀，禮金數字最好是雙數，表示成雙成對。若是為人祝壽，或慶祝學業有成、喜獲麟兒等，也是用紅包袋來包現金餽贈。任何雙數的禮金數字都可以，除了 4 以外，因為 4 的中文讀音很接近「死」，所以即便 4 是偶數，也不可以出現在喜事的禮金行列，因為是大家避之唯恐不及的忌諱。若是出席喪禮，通常會用白色的信封袋裝單數開頭的禮金，比如 1100 元或是 3100 元，表示形單影隻，甚表哀戚。

　　至於禮物的忌諱，則是不可將時鐘、掛鐘等作為送人的禮物，因為「送鐘」與「送終」的讀音完全一樣，而送終是為離世的人送別，會有詛咒別人的意思，因此不可不慎。另一忌諱則是送人雨傘，因為「傘」的讀音類似「散」，有曲終人散的含意，因此擔心會帶來不吉利。同理，若去醫院探病，想送新鮮水果給病人，千萬不可送梨子，因為「梨」與「離」的讀音一樣，表示離開人世，在醫院裡尤其被視為不吉祥的象徵。

　　最後，人們收到禮物時通常不會馬上拆開，而是等事後私下再開，就算是在眾人面前打開禮物，也會很斯文地慢慢打開，以盡量不破壞外包裝的美麗為最高準則。像這些臺灣人習以為常的送禮文化，卻也常讓外國友人嘖嘖稱奇。

Red envelopes for weddings

8.3 Gifting Culture

• •

Like many countries, Taiwan is a country where giving gifts is very popular and, at times, necessary. People prepare and present gifts on many occasions. During important life events such as getting married or having a newborn, people receive and send gifts to honor the occasions. There are some rules, however, that locals follow for the gifting practice in Taiwan.

When invited to a wedding, guests would bring monetary gifts to the bride

Giving a pocket watch as a gift – a taboo

and the groom enclosed in a red envelope with various auspicious blessings inscribed. Red is considered a color of good fortune and happiness. For joyful occasions such as weddings or graduations, be sure to include denominations that begin with an even number. Odd numbers do not make perfect pairs and, therefore, are considered unlucky. Only at funerals will people prepare monetary gifts of odd-number denominations in a white, instead of a red, envelope. However, one even number, "four" (sì 四), is taboo because its pronunciation in Mandarin resembles the word "death." Red envelopes containing congratulatory gifts will never have denominations that begin with "four," as it means bad luck. In fact, many hospitals and hotels in Taiwan do not have a fourth floor simply because no one would want to stay there due to the inference.

Some gifts are considered major taboos in Taiwanese culture. Clocks, be it wall clocks or desk clocks, are never given as a gift because the pronunciation "clock" (zhōng 鐘) in Mandarin, when combined with the word "give" (sòng 送), sounds the same as seeing someone off to the end of his or her life. Umbrellas (sǎn 傘) are another taboo gift because the Mandarin pronunciation of umbrella sounds very similar to that of "breakup" (sàn 散). If gifted to a friend, an umbrella could be interpreted as a curse to the friendship.

Unlike many Westerners who would open their gifts right in front of the gift senders, Taiwanese people would rather wait until they have left. Even when they do open their gifts publicly, say, at a birthday party, they would not rip apart the wrapping paper of a present like many Westerners would do. Instead, they would take the time to carefully open the gift while keeping the gift packaging almost intact. Careful unwrapping of a present is considered a respectful gesture to the sender.

Bride and groom with the "double-happiness" character

8.4 婚禮習俗

　　臺灣的婚禮習俗很繁複，大多都與趨吉避凶有關。紅色是婚禮傳統的顏色，代表吉祥，婚禮中的主色，不管是新人的禮服或是婚禮會場的布置，以及賓客的穿著，都最好有紅色，才不會冒犯成婚的新人與他們的家庭。但近年西風東漸，很多結婚的新人選擇西方的白色作為婚禮的主色，在服裝上或婚禮會場若都沒有任何紅色的物件出現，也慢慢被許多家庭接受。

　　在婚禮當天，有一定的迎娶行程。首先，新郎的家庭會出動車隊到女方家迎娶新娘，車隊通常是二輛車或六輛車，隨行的人數也一定要是雙數才吉利。抵達女方家時，女方家人會先放鞭炮歡迎新郎的車隊來臨。新郎必須接受女方家人或好友出的難題，迎刃而解後才算通過考驗，得以見到新娘。隨後新郎新娘便要拜別父母，二人一起在新娘的父母前叩頭，感謝新娘父母的養育之恩，並允諾要好好照顧彼此，不讓父母擔心。

等到良辰吉時來臨，就會結束迎娶的過程，離開新娘的家，前往宴客處。新娘一旦出了室外，家人必須為她撐把黑傘，原因是要避開天神的光芒，因為老天爺是最崇高的神祇，但在新人的大喜之日，新娘的光芒卻有可能壓過天神的光彩，所以為了不讓天神失色，必須用一把大的黑傘或米篩把新娘的耀眼光彩略為遮蓋，待新娘進入車內或室內後即可解除對天神的威脅。

載著新人的禮車也會精心裝飾，在車頭會別上大的花環，車門把也會別上小花束。最重要的是，會綁著一根甘蔗梗在車邊，車子發動駛離前，新娘會搖下車窗，將一把扇子丟出車外，甘蔗的甘甜代表了要說好話，扇子則代表要捨棄壞脾氣。車子駛離後，新娘的父母會將準備好的一盆水潑出，象徵新人要丟棄所有的壞習氣，開始人生的新頁。

接著新人會前往婚禮會場。在臺灣，除非是宗教性質的婚禮會在教堂舉行，一般人都是在飯店或餐廳舉行婚禮及婚宴，有些迎娶儀式也在飯店完成。結婚典禮完成後，即會前往新人的新家。抵達新家時，新娘會先過火盆、踩瓦，象徵破除過往的陋習，以建立嶄新家庭。新郎的父母及長輩，會坐在大廳裡由新娘奉茶，代表家裡新進成員對父母的孝敬。最後要送入洞房前，會讓一位小男孩兒去新人的床上「滾床」，以帶來好運勢，讓新人趕快報喜受孕，成為爸媽。

8.4 Wedding Traditions

Weddings are among the most culturally-specific activities that embody many social values and customs. In general, weddings in Taiwan take on Western-style white gowns and black tuxedos. More and more newlyweds, however, would like to dress in traditional wedding gowns in red, which is considered the optimal color for all social events in Taiwan. Regardless of a couple's preference for Western-style or traditional garments, there is a set procedure to follow on the wedding date.

In the morning on the wedding day, the groom's family will arrange a motorcade to arrive at the bride's house. The motorcade consists of either two or six vehicles carrying an even number of members, including the groom. Each ceremonial vehicle is decorated with a bridal wreath at the front of the car and a red ribbon on each door handle.

As the motorcade approaches the bride's house, the procession will set off firecrackers to announce the arrival of the groom's party. After entering the house, the groom will receive a series of challenges from bridesmaids. Only when successfully passing the challenges will the groom be able to see the bride. Then the bride will offer and serve sweet tea to the groom as well as her own parents. Together the couple will pay tribute to the Heavens and ancestors with sticks of incense.

The highlight of the ceremony occurs when the couple kneels and bows to the bride's parents, thanking them for raising their girl into a beautiful

A bride tossing a paper fan letting go of bad temper

woman. They will also receive blessings and words of wisdom from the bride's parents. This is the moment when a bride may shed tears as she is no longer under her parents' wing and expected to build a family of her own.

Then comes the opportune time to leave the bride's home. The groom will accompany the bride, with her veil on, to step outside the house. As they exit, the matchmaker will hold a rice sieve or a black umbrella to shadow the bride's head. It is said that a bride on her wedding day possesses an almighty spirit, possibly outshining the heaven's. And yet it will not be acceptable to outrival the gods under any circumstances. Therefore, a sieve or an umbrella provides a buffer between the bride and Heaven.

As the groom leads the bride into their wedding limousine, a stalk of sugar

Tea serving to the in-laws

A typical wedding banquet table setup

cane prepared by the bride's family will be tied along the car's roof, reminding the bride to "sweeten up" her in-laws. Before departing, the bride will roll down the window and toss a paper fan out of the car, a symbol of abandoning any temperamental traits in exchange for "kindness" (shàn 善), which has the same pronunciation as the word "fan" (shàn 扇) in Mandarin. As the car is leaving, the parents of the bride will prepare a bucket of water and splash the water on the ground behind the vehicle, symbolizing no looking back and cementing a determination to start a new page of her life.

After leaving the bride's house, the couple then heads to the wedding ceremony. In Taiwan, wedding ceremonies usually take place in luxurious restaurants or hotels. Unless it's a religious wedding that will occur in a church, many people in Taiwan usually host their wedding ceremonies in locations where the wedding banquets will be held. During the ceremony, the couple will be married by, instead of a religious leader, someone who is well-respected or significant to them. After exchanging their wedding vows and rings, the bride and the groom will be united as witnessed by the wedding guests.

As the newlyweds arrive at their new home afterward, the matchmaker will again use a rice sieve or a black umbrella to shield the bride from the Heavens. Before entering the front door, the bride should cross over a burning fire pot and step on a piece of clay tile to crush it, expelling all her bad habits from the past. Once the couple enters the house, they will worship gods and the groom's ancestors with incense sticks. Parents of the groom will be waiting in the hall to welcome their new family member. The bride will hold a tea tray and serve tea to each member of the groom's family. The couple would then proceed to enter their bridal chamber, where they will drink to a toast with their arms intertwined. The last part of the ceremony usually involves a little boy rolling over on the couple's bed, a good luck charm believed to bring a boy's birth to the newlyweds in the near future.

Despite all the traditional rituals and customs associated with weddings, many young couples nowadays opt for a simplified procedure and may skip some of the activities described above.

8.5 冥婚

　　冥婚是指死人之間、生人與死人之間的婚姻結合。《周禮》上記載：「禁遷葬者與嫁殤者。」表示當時有此社會習俗，而儒家思想是反對此舉的。雖然儒家學說反對冥婚，但卻未能完全禁止冥婚的風俗。華人普遍認為亡靈若有遺憾，鬼魂會讓仍在世的家人不安，甚至帶來霉運。若有單身女子亡故，臺灣傳統思想中，認為單身女子並不屬於原生家庭，過世後也無法列入祖先牌位，接受後代祭祠。女子必須經過嫁娶，進入夫家，才能列於夫家的家族牌位中。所以，單身即過世的「孤娘」，必須透過冥婚找到夫家，才能接受夫家香火，不致在冥界淒涼地孤老。

　　臺灣盛行的冥婚稱「娶神主」，儀式雖與一般結婚儀式類似，卻是生人與死人之間的嫁娶。當一名單身女性逝世，她的家人可能會放一些紅包在路上，等待有緣男性撿起紅包。這些紅包裡面可能有現金、紙錢、死者的頭髮或指甲等。如果拾獲者不願配合，可能會因此招來厄運，所以很多臺灣男性從小便被教導，不要隨意撿起地上的紅包袋。隨著臺灣的教育普及，女性經濟亦趨獨立，必須透過婚姻才能得到社會認可的觀念已經慢慢在改變，但冥婚的習俗仍然存在臺灣社會的許多角落，主要的原因無非是為了讓逝者的靈魂得到安息，也讓生者感到安慰，放下心中的牽掛。

8.5 Posthumous Marriage

When a strong earthquake hit Tainan on February 6, 2016, a building that nearly collapsed caused more than a hundred deaths. A man trapped inside the building was found miraculously alive after more than 55 hours under the debris. However, his girlfriend nearby was not as fortunate and did not survive by the time the rescue team found her. The couple had been in love for a long time, and tying the knot was just a matter of time. The man, saddened by his beloved woman's tragic death, wanted to marry her in a posthumous wedding. He said he didn't want his girlfriend to be lonely in the underworld and wanted her to be part of his family by marrying her. The news story became an instant headline in every newspaper the following day in Taiwan.

A posthumous marriage like the case above is not uncommon in Taiwan. There are two types of posthumous marriages: two deceased persons married by their family members or one living person with a deceased person. The rationale behind posthumous marriage is complex. Some people believe a posthumous wedding that announces the official union between two people in love would make the one who experienced an untimely death rest in peace. Traditionally in Taiwan, financially independent single women are considered a stand-alone social unit. Unless they get married and adopt their husbands' family names, they are no longer part of their birth families. If a single woman dies too early, she cannot be buried in the family cemetery. Instead, these women would be buried alone without belonging to any family. Under the circumstances, the deceased woman's family will try to plan a posthumous wedding for her to belong to a family in the eyes of Heaven. If a couple has been in love before both of them die in a tragic accident, their families would consider organizing a posthumous wedding to allow them to stay together in another world. If one of them dies unexpectedly, especially for the woman who dies single, the deceased's family would ask their beloved to grant the favor of a posthumous marriage. A ceremony is performed so that their living families would have closure, knowing the deceased's soul would be attached to their partner's family.

But how do they find a posthumous partner for a deceased woman who had been single and unattached? The deceased woman's family will place inside a red envelope a string of her hair, a piece of her nail, and a card with her birthdate. The family would then put the envelope on a busy sidewalk with many passersby. The first man who picks up the red envelope will be approached by the family members hiding nearby. He will be asked to marry the woman posthumously since he is the "destined" partner chosen by the deceased woman. Those who refuse are doomed to encounter dreadful luck afterward as the deceased woman will hold grudges against the man for a while. This is why boys, especially in the southern part of Taiwan where posthumous marriage is more prevalent, are long taught not to pick up any red envelopes on the streets.

There is a news article about a young Westerner married to a Taiwanese wife and incidentally picked up a red envelope while walking down the streets. Immediately, he was surrounded by several people nearby asking him to marry their dearly departed daughter. The man furiously refused and walked away, leaving the sad family even more depressed. "I wish I could help." the Westerner replied, "but I'm already happily married. What was I supposed to do?"

Posthumous marriage is a cultural practice still accepted in many parts of Taiwan. As women in Taiwan become more educated and financially independent, more and more families are beginning to embrace the idea that daughters do not necessarily need marriage to affirm their social status. But just in case if you are a visitor to Taiwan and stumble upon a red envelope on the sidewalks someday, do not pick it up unless you are ready to be united with a deceased spirit!

8.6 算命文化

　　臺灣人承襲了華人喜歡算命的習慣，不論事情大小，不論年齡高低，都可以想方設法算命，舉凡面相、手相、塔羅牌、星座、紫微斗數、鳥卦等都是常見的算命方式。算命的地點也隨處可見，尤其在香火鼎盛的廟宇附近最容易有算命的業者聚集，例如在大臺北地區的二個著名廟宇——行天宮與龍山寺，因為到廟中求籤祈福的善男信女經常順道光顧，附近已經有很成熟的算命商圈在蓬勃的發展。這些算命業者與捷運地下街商場結合，不但環境明亮整潔，也很重算命客戶的隱私需求，每一位命理老師幾乎都是執業超過十年的師父，為很多徬徨無助的客人指點迷津。因為這二個算命商圈已經做出國內外的口碑，吸引了很多國際觀光客前來，命理師父也漸漸地國際化，能以外語執行算命過程的溝通與說明，目前許多算命師皆能操英語、日語、韓語。

　　除了收費型態的算命，還有免費的廟宇求籤。只要有廟宇，就會有民眾去求神問卜，因此大多數臺灣的廟宇，都在祭壇香爐附近設有籤筒。求問事時，民眾要先在心中默念想問神明的事，隨後在籤筒中抽竹籤，依竹籤的指示去找對應的籤文，而籤文都是古詩詞，需要解籤才能了解籤文背後的涵義。通常廟宇裡都會安排解籤的服務，讓民眾詢問，雖然是免費的服務，但民眾在得到籤文解釋後，廟方都會請求籤人捐獻香火錢，這樣的形式與基督教教堂在作禮拜後，尋求教友的捐獻有幾分相似。

　　隨著臺灣越來越國際化，人民的生活環境也越來越便利、都會化，但物質生活的現代化，似乎沒有讓人民免於憂慮，反倒是快速的工作與生活步調讓人神經緊繃，對未來的不確定感提高，因而使算命行業更加蓬勃發展，帶來臺灣算命大街的興起與繁榮。

Palm reading

8.6 Fortune-telling

• •

If you stop a random pedestrian in Taiwan and ask if they have been to a fortune-teller anytime in their life, chances are many of them have. Fortune-telling is very much a part of people's life in Taiwan that very few adults have never had the experience. People consult fortune-tellers for all kinds of reasons, ranging from what to name their newborn babies, when to move into a new house, how to fix a troubled business, what numbers to buy for lottery tickets, or where to bury their deceased families, to name a few. There

Street of Fortune Telling in Taipei

A bilingual fortune teller's stand

are also various methods of performing fortune-telling, such as astrology, Tarot cards, palm reading, face reading, bird divination, and name analysis, etc. The list goes on and on. Moreover, fortune-telling can be found in many venues, including, but not limited to, private businesses, night markets, temples, or underground shopping areas near metro stops. Because people seek advice from fortune-tellers at such a considerable scale, the fortune-telling business stays vibrant in Taiwan.

An old Chinese saying goes: "Fate comes first, luck second, Fengshui third, virtue fourth, and education fifth." (一 命、 二 運、三風水、四積德、五讀書) (Discover Taipei, 2012). Despite conditions predetermined at birth, there are still many other factors that we can maneuver to change the course of our lives. Fengshui means how we arrange our space and surroundings. Virtue concerns the good deeds we attempt. Education points to our efforts and passion for learning. The last three factors are definitely subject to human discipline and determination, while the first two are much less controllable. However, it is the second factor, luck, that gives fortune telling maneuvering room. When people have done everything within their power and still cannot be happy with the results, they would more likely seek help from fortune-telling. Also, people's desire to reduce the uncertainty about the future prompts them to seek advice from augury. If they could avoid some hurdles through divination advice, they would do anything to gain insights from a fortune-teller.

Two very different areas surround the two famous temples in Taipei with an abundance of fortune-telling businesses. Xingtian Temple (行天宮), located in Taipei's hustle and bustle, is one of the city's most prominent temples. In the nearby metro stop, the entire underpass area houses the Xingtian Temple Fortune Telling Street (行天宮命理大街). More than 20 fortune-teller stands are in the area, many of which have been in business for over a decade. These fortune tellers provide a variety of services, some as affordable as NT$500 each session. They have attracted foreign tourists who come to Xingtian Temple for some sightseeing. In recent years, some of the fortune-

Bird Divination fortune telling

Fortune-telling bamboo sticks in a temple

tellers offer sessions in Japanese to serve the Japanese tourists.

The other famous temple in Taipei is Longshan Temple (龍山寺), a much older temple established in 1738 during the Qing Dynasty. Longshan

Fortune-telling scripts ready for interpretation

Temple Underground Shopping Bazaar (龍山寺地下商城) is now the largest fortune telling street in Taipei, hosting more than 30 booths of diviners. Among the various fortune telling techniques used by these masters, bird divination is a unique routine that involves a live bird's collaboration. When a customer approaches a fortune teller with questions, the fortune teller would ask the seeker to ask the questions silently in his/her mind. The master would then open the birdcage, in front of which a pile of divination cards is placed. The well-trained bird, instead of flying around once out of the cage, rather would stand still and look into the stack of divination cards, from which the bird will pick out three. The three divination cards, each with a poem and a colorful picture, will represent the seeker's past, present, and future. The master's interpretation of the three cards is key to understanding the message hidden within the cards. A fortune teller using this technique can say shockingly accurate things about the seeker's past and present status, thereby gaining trust from the seeker before offering guidance for their future encounters. These masters are often visited by celebrities in show business seeking career advice. Like the fortune-telling practitioners in the Xingtian Temple neighborhood, many would conduct their divination in foreign languages such as English, Japanese, or Korean for tourists.

Another common practice among Taiwanese locals is drawing bamboo sticks at a temple after contemplating the questions silently to the gods worshipped in the temple (Harper, 2018). People would walk into a temple and pray right in front of the gods' statues while silently asking their questions. They would then turn to a container of bamboo sticks next to the altar, where they are to pick just one from among hundreds of sticks at random. The chosen stick would indicate where to find the corresponding box of scripts. These scripts are usually ancient texts or poems which require interpretations regarding the questions at hand. Each temple is generally set up with a counter for script interpretation. Someone familiar with all the available texts can address each seeker's request at no cost! When the interpretation is completed, the seeker will be invited to make a donation of any amount to the temple, much like how tithes are paid to Christian churches. No donations, however, will ever be forced upon seekers of guidance in temples.

Fortune telling has been an ancient practice throughout history in Chinese cultures. In Taiwan, the ancient tradition continues to thrive despite modernization in rapid-paced life. Modernization and urbanization may have helped people to enjoy better living conditions. People's fear of uncertainty has not changed much and may have even polarized due to stress from work and life. This explains why people frequently seek assurance or guidance from fortune-tellers and why the business thrives in Taiwan.

8.7 禁忌與迷信

世界上所有的文化都有禁忌與迷信，臺灣也不例外。這些世代流傳下來的文化禁忌也許基於對大自然或鬼神的敬畏，也許基於科技不發達時，人類自我保護的機制，不論如何，透過了解這些習俗背後的社會歷史典故，能讓我們理解每一個禁忌或迷信背後都有一定的文化意涵，也讓外來文化的人有所依循，不致在無意間冒犯了本地人而不自知。

Putting chopsticks vertical in rice is a taboo

8.7 Taboos and Superstitions

Each culture has its taboos and superstitions. There are many cultural taboos and superstitions in Taiwan as well. Many of them are based on beliefs passed from generation to generation.

Do not Point at the Moon.

Children learn not to point at the Moon because it is considered disrespectful. Ancestors believed that the Moon Goddess, who resides in the moon, looks after all creatures in the world. In the agricultural era, farmers would rise with the Sun in the morning and rest at dusk. Tribal people, particularly the Bunun tribe (布農族), would farm according to the moon's waxing and waning phases. Their ancestors believed that Moon would shy away when pointed by people. When Moon "disappeared" from the sky, as we now know the result of a lunar eclipse, ancestors attributed it to offensive human acts and linked it to a drought or a famine. Children are taught to be in awe of the Moon. Pointing at the Moon, especially a crescent moon that shapes like a sickle, could result in losing an ear during one's sleep. To the present day, pointing at the Moon remains taboo in Taiwan.

Chopsticks Manners

It is taboo to stick chopsticks vertically into a bowl of rice during a meal. Only offerings for ancestors or spirits have chopsticks inserted into their rice bowls. A living person doing so would likely invite bad luck or unwanted spirits to consume the rice. A guest to someone's house doing so during the meal means a curse to the host. The proper way to place a pair of chopsticks during a meal is to either put on a chopstick rest, if there is one; or place it horizontally on the rim of a rice bowl. Better yet, simply put the chopsticks on the table next to the rice bowl, but never stick them upright in the rice.

Names in Red Ink

Do not write people's names in red ink. In ancient times, those on death row would have their names written in red ink when the time of execution came. People believe that any person in the living world would live to a pre-determined age trackable by the King of the Underworld (yán luó wáng 閻羅王). When the time has come to summon those back to his realm, the King would use red ink to circle those names. Therefore, it is taboo to mark a living person's name in red ink because it would indicate the end of the person's life. Although red is a lucky color in many social occasions in Taiwan, names written in red symbolize "blood" or misfortune and should be treated with caution.

Whistling at Night

Whistling at night would likely attract ghosts nearby. The pitch of a whistling sound is said to attract wandering spirits at night. Ghosts could follow the whistler home and cause bad luck. During the seventh lunar month, the Ghost Month, ghosts from the underworld are free to walk the Earth. They remain hidden in the dark corners during the day and

Great Fortune With You

一路發

"Non-stop prosperity" in Mandarin

become active at night. A whistling sound could gather the roaming ghosts unintentionally and invite them home.

Indoor Umbrellas

Do not open an umbrella indoors. Umbrellas, when open, can capture evil spirits when used by experienced exorcists. An open umbrella in the room may attract ghosts to hide under and invite the ghosts to stay in the house. Another belief that causes the taboo is that children who carry an open umbrella indoors would not grow taller. An open umbrella may symbolically act as a lid suppressing a child's growth. Scientifically, it is probably more of a safety concern that an open umbrella used as a toy by children could cause harm. Parents simply use the taboo to warn children against playing with an open umbrella in the house.

Lucky "Six" and "Eight"

The number 6 and the number 8 are the two digits most frequently used to customize a lottery ticket in Taiwan. It shows how popular they are. People consider the number 6 lucky because there is an idiom "Six plus six makes perfection" (liù liù dà shùn 六六大順). In general, even numbers are considered lucky in Taiwanese culture, except number 4, which sounds similar to the word "death." Two sixes, totaling twelve, mean an abundance of good luck. Unlike how the number 666 is representative of Satan in the West, any repetition of 6 is a lucky number in Taiwan. In fact, it is very common to spot a car in the streets with a vanity license plate number containing 6666, requiring an additional fee to obtain such a plate. The number 8 is also trendy among Taiwanese lottery players. The pronunciation of 8 (bā 八) in Mandarin sounds very close to the pronunciation of prosperity (fā 發). The figure 168, when pronounced in Mandarin (yī lù fā 一路發), goes even one step further to mean "nonstop prosperity."

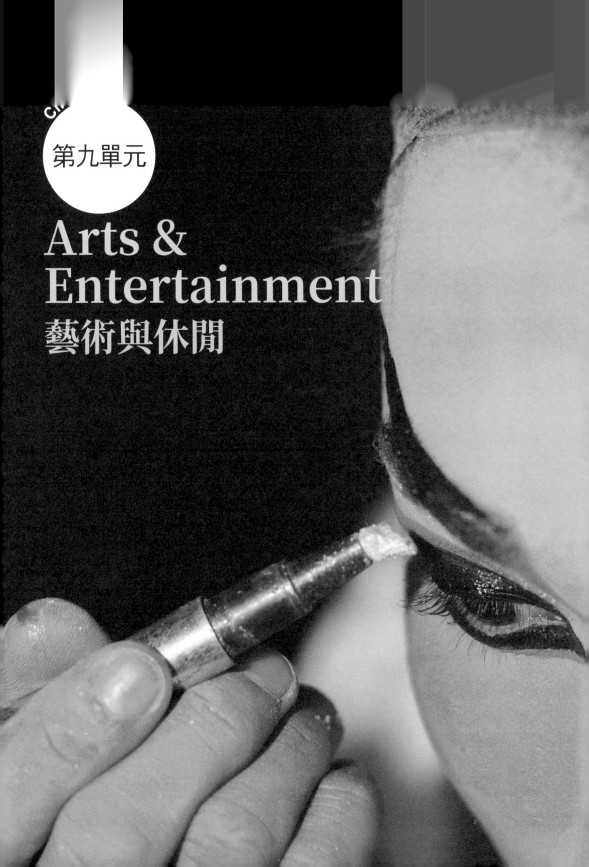

第九單元

Arts & Entertainment
藝術與休閒

9.1 雲門舞集

　　雲門舞集是由林懷民在 1973 年創辦的臺灣第一個現代舞蹈表演團體。「雲門」的由來是根據《呂氏春秋》中的一句話「黃帝時,大容作雲門,大卷……」,以炎黃子孫的老祖宗黃帝時代的舞蹈命名,來紀念最古老的謝天祭祖舞蹈。

　　雲門舞集的舞作取材甚廣,包括古典文學、民間故事、臺灣歷史、社會現象的衍化發揮,乃至前衛觀念的嘗試。林懷民的編舞更是融合了西方的現代舞、東方的京劇戲曲、太極、氣功、冥想等元素。創作之初的舞作如《薪傳》、《流浪者之歌》、《家族合唱》等皆發想於歷史社會事件,反映了臺灣社會的現況與國際處境。多年來隨著人民與社會的進步,舞作內容更包羅萬象,開發更多元的創作空間。藉由雲門的發展也可一窺臺灣社會的變革,在國際社會中,雲門儼然已成為臺灣的另一個代名詞。

Legacy (Courtesy of David Yu)

9.1 Cloud Gate Dance Theatre

In 1973, Lin Hwai-min (林懷民) established the first contemporary dance group in Taiwan at the age of 26. Being the oldest of five children from an affluent family, Lin grew up nurturing his classical music and literary interests. By the age of 22, Lin had published a book of short stories to showcase his writing talent and was offered a fellowship to the International Writing Program at the University of Iowa the following year. While studying literature in the U.S., he became interested in choreography, to which his parents were opposed. They considered dancing a hobby rather than a profession or a career. At the time, there wasn't any professional dance group in Taiwan. People simply could not fathom a dancing career for their children. Despite his parents' opposition, Lin founded the Cloud Gate Dance Group upon returning to Taiwan and became a progenitor of modern dance in his homeland.

The name of the dance group, "Cloud Gate" (雲門), came from the oldest dance in Han history, as documented in The Annals of Lu's Commentaries of History (呂氏春秋). The book was written by Buwei Lu (呂不韋), a prime minister during the Qin Emperor's sovereignty, in 241 BCE. According to the book, the common ancestor for all Chinese people, Xuanyuan Huangdi (xuān yuan huáng dì 軒轅黃帝), "Yellow Emperor," ordered a dance performance to glorify the swirling clouds in honor of the blessings from ancestors and gods. The oldest dance, "Cloud Gate," signified one's gratitude and appreciation for the natural surroundings and the ancestral protection.

Similarly, Lin named the first modern dance group in Taiwan "Cloud Gate" to pay tribute to the origin of dance in Han history.

While studying in the U.S., Lin took classes at the Martha Graham School in New York and later cited influence from Paul Taylor, Merce Cunningham, and José Limón. To reflect his Taiwanese upbringing and Western influences, Lin has choreographed his work by blending elements from Western modern dance, classical ballet, Chinese folk dance, Tai-Chi, and meditation. Cloud Gate's first production "*The Tale of the White Serpent*" (白 蛇 傳) in 1975, based on a popular Chinese folk story often seen in Peking Opera, successfully fused the modern dance techniques and theatrical concepts from the East and the West. In later years, a trilogy of works (行草三部曲), *Cursive* (行 草 2001), *Cursive II* (行 草 貳 2002), and *Wild Cursive* (狂 草 2005), is a series of artistic transformations inspired by a particular style of Chinese calligraphy. Regardless of the various calligraphy styles, Lin perceives that all calligraphers' brushes would "dance" on the rice paper as they write. Dancers interpret the energy and movements involved in each calligraphic stroke before transforming them into meditative aesthetics on stage.

Besides the theatrical and artistic presentation, Cloud Gate also incorporates Taiwanese cultural underpinnings into its works, especially those crucial moments in Taiwan's history. After retreating from Mainland China to Taiwan in 1949, the Taiwanese regime led by Chiang Kai-shek had been butting heads with the Communist government in China and was eventually expelled from the United Nations in 1971. When Lin established the Cloud Gate Dance Theatre in 1973, the island was at the crossroads of searching for its own roots and identity. "*Legacy*" (薪傳 1978) depicts the hardships

Legacy (Courtesy of David Yu)

Portrait of the Families (Courtesy of David Yu)

settlers from Mainland China experienced. "*Songs of the Wanderers*" (流浪 者之歌 1994) uses the imagery of a Buddhist monk standing under a stream of falling rice as a symbolic act to contemplate Taiwan's identity amidst international solitude (Wroe, 2016). "*Portrait of the Families*" (家 族 合 唱 1997) addresses the social turmoil and the massacre of intellectuals during the martial law period from 1949 to 1987. It was only after martial law had been lifted could the taboo of White Terror be unveiled years later.

Since its establishment, Cloud Gate has in many ways helped shape Taiwan's self-identity and emerged as a national icon, both domestically and internationally. Its works reflect the social changes that people in Taiwan have experienced and the collective memory that Taiwanese society has come to embrace. The symbolic representation of the art form helps elevate Taiwan's spirituality to higher ground.

Songs of the Wanderers (Courtesy of David Yu)

9.2 歌仔戲

　　歌仔戲最早的起源是宜蘭蘭陽平原上務農的老百姓在農作之餘的哼歌表演，通常在廟會的時候搭著戲棚子演出。台上的人粉墨登場，唱戲耍槍跑龍套，台下的人鼓掌吆喝叫好，在那個沒有電視或任何聲光娛樂的年代，看歌仔戲是大家最享受的休閒活動。後來受到京劇的影響，慢慢地加入了服裝、化妝、角色、劇情等元素，歌仔戲逐漸展現它風華絕代的一面，在臺灣發光發熱。

　　有了生、旦、淨、丑的角色，還有唱、念、演、打的舞台技巧，歌仔戲的表演者必須具備舞台劇、音樂劇、雜耍團的十八般武藝，才能勝任一齣劇的演出，因此很多歌仔戲的優秀表演者都是學徒出身，慢慢累積舞台經驗，才能在台上精彩呈現這門藝術。歌仔戲完全以臺語唱作，取材自本土的歌謠與典故，是真正道地的臺灣藝術創作，因為許多藝術團體的多年耕耘，臺灣歌仔戲的表演團體，已經名揚國際，為臺灣的本土藝術再添新頁。

Taiwanese Opera performers on stage

9.2 Taiwanese Opera

Taiwanese opera is a form of traditional art performed during temple festivals in Taiwan. It originated from the Langyang Plain (蘭陽平原), Yilan County in the northeast of Taiwan over a century ago. Farming folks were humming tunes in the form of a minor opera when they worked in the field. These tunes later evolved into songs honoring gods during temple events. At a time when television sets were a household luxury, watching a Taiwanese opera in the plaza of a temple was the best entertainment for rural farmers. The lines and songs are all delivered in Taiwanese. The opera had story elements based

A martial male character

on folk tales. In the beginning, no costumes or makeup were present. Over time the opera evolved into grand opera, adopting many features from Peking Opera. Glamorous costumes and makeup styles were added to the production of the opera.

In addition to the elaborate costumes and splendid makeup, there are also four types of roles in each performance. Each of these roles has its distinct function. First, Shēng (生) means male leads among which there are senior males – Lǎo shēng (老生), young males – Hsiǎo shēng (小生), and martial males – Wǔ shēng (武 生). The second type of role is female leads – Dàn (旦), which further breaks down into four groups: ingénues (小 旦), grande dames (老 旦), coquettes (花旦), and doleful females (苦旦). Jìng (淨), the third type of role, refers to deified male historical figures such as Guan Gong (關 公) the fearless General or Bao Gong (包 公) the legendary Judge. Finally, the fourth type of role is Chǒu (丑), the jesters. Different characters would also carry distinctive props. For example, a character with a folding fan would definitely be the young male lead (小生). In contrast, a leading ingénue (小旦) would likely carry a handkerchief or a floating fan. Their costumes, postures, gestures, and makeup will also reveal their roles in the performance.

Characters on stage would speak, sing, act, and perform stunts, the four performing Taiwanese opera techniques. These operas fuse a multitude of performance arts in a singular production: Performers need to remember their lines and act out the story like actors and actresses in a play; The artists need to know how to sing their dialogue just like singers in a musical. Finally, they need to perform aerobatic moves, especially among the martial male characters, just like gymnasts but donned with heavy headpieces and costumes. All these performing techniques demand years of practice and experience on the performers. Many Taiwanese Opera performers start their careers at a young age as apprentices and slowly work their way up to the top of the profession.

The stage production involves a lot of technical support. For example, whenever two martial male characters begin an aerobatic fight on stage, the live music from drums and gongs, along with the dazzling lighting effects, offers the audience a visual sensation, leaving them in awe. The cheers from the crowd also give the performers instant feedback. When Taiwanese Opera was only available as an outdoor event during temple festivals, people congregated to enjoy the shows. These shows normally drew a massive crowd. Therefore, some theatre managers began to invite the performing troupes to theatrical performances, opening the door to new possibilities.

One unique feature of Taiwanese Opera is its seven-word tune. A piece of singing consists of four lines and seven words in each line. The seven-word tune is the hallmark of Taiwanese Opera. If an opera does not have a seven-word tune, it couldn't be considered as Taiwanese Opera. During the 1950s, major Taiwanese radio stations invited several performing opera groups to record and broadcast their performances on-air. This allowed the opera troupes to enrich their sound repertoire further as radio could only deliver music and dialogues via the airwaves.

In 1962, Taiwanese Opera officially appeared on the screen when the Taiwan Television Enterprise (TTV) was established. By the late 1980s, Taiwanese Opera had evolved into a prominent symbol of Taiwanese cultural art. At its peak, Taiwanese Opera would take up all the prime time TV programs every night. The singing and choreography components of the performance had included more techniques from Western opera. The costumes and settings had become even more glamourous and theatre-worthy. Many Taiwanese Opera troupes have now achieved international fame. Despite social tension during the Japanese colonial rule and the martial law era, Taiwanese Opera has come very far to maintain its vitality and is a good representation of homegrown theatre in Taiwan.

9.3 布袋戲

　　布袋戲最早是在十七世紀左右，由中國福建省的移民帶入臺灣。本來是在廟宇特殊慶典時才會安排演出，演出的內容皆是人民熟知的忠孝節義故事，但加上了掌戲人的旁白與操控的動作，布偶頓時就被賦予了生命，有喜怒哀樂，能眉目傳情，許多經典人物如史艷文、素還真等膾炙人口，到今天都仍享有廣大的粉絲支持。

　　而成就布袋戲成功與否的背後靈魂人物就是掌戲人，李天祿是臺灣布袋戲文化的重量級先驅，他將布袋戲從市井小民的休閒娛樂，提昇為足以代表臺灣在地文化的藝術表演，並多次受邀到國際場合介紹臺灣的布袋戲，為這項傳統藝術帶來國際能見度。隨著科技的演進，布袋戲得以結合更多元的風貌，繼續生生不息地向前邁進。

Pili Puppet Theatre exhibition

9.3 Taiwanese Hand Puppetry

Taiwanese Hand Puppetry, pronounced "bù dài xì" (布袋戲) in Mandarin and "potehi" in Taiwanese, originated in the Fujian Province of China and was brought to Taiwan by Fujian migrants during the 17th century. Bù dài xì or potehi means "cloth bag drama" verbatim. Each puppet has a wooden head exquisitely carved and wooden hands that can hold objects and is donned with beautifully embroidered clothing. Because a puppeteer would wear a hand puppet like a glove, it's also called Glove Puppetry. A puppeteer would insert a thumb into one hand of the puppet, an index finger into the hollow head, and the rest of the fingers into the other hand of the puppet, allowing the puppeteer to easily control the puppet's movements, including nodding, clapping, walking, pointing, etc. The puppet show is performed on a colorful stage, behind which there are puppeteers, narrators, and musicians. Typically, the puppeteer would also be the narrator to sound out the storyline and dialogues.

The making of a puppet involves delicate craftsmanship. A puppet's head is carved out of a solid block of wood, and the carving process can take days to complete. The carved head is then glued with layers of paper before applying a final coating of clay. The head's production is the costliest step, both in terms of time and money, and can take up to three months for 20 layers of paper to dry and settle into shape. Each puppet's facial features, down to the eyelashes, are all handcrafted to look life-like. The wooden hands of each puppet have fingers that can hold miniature weapons or cups

Classic character Sù Huán Zhēn

Handmade hand puppets

when necessary. Finally, each piece of clothing requires intricate embroidery and final assembly with the head and hands.

During the 1970s, the stage-performed hand puppet shows made it to the TV screen and were broadcast live. Additional sound effects, moving features, smoke, and other special effects were added to the TV production. Since then, fight scenes between two puppets have become particularly intense and popular as puppeteers would demonstrate their superb skills to engage the puppets into a battle using miniature weapons held in their hands. It is among those fabulous tricks that a puppet, tossed by the puppeteer high up in the air, would land right onto the puppeteer's hand after completing an aerial somersault. Other amazing tricks, seemingly done by the puppets, include balancing spinning plates, juggling a rod, using a folding fan, or shooting arrows. A well-manipulated puppet could fool viewers into thinking that it has come to life.

Hand Puppetry shows first started as temple events to celebrate Buddha's birthday. Stories of puppet shows were usually folklore that people knew very well. Early settlers from China, who spoke the Fujian Hokkien dialect, now called Taiwanese, felt close to home as they watched the puppet shows performed in Taiwanese. As the performance evolved over the years and became a national art in Taiwan, more and more foreigners could appreciate the "theatre on a palm" (zhǎng zhōng xì 掌中戲) presented by hand puppet shows. In 1993, "*The Puppetmaster*," a film directed by now world-famous Hou, Hsiao-Hsien (侯 孝 賢), depicts the life and contribution of a master puppeteer, Li, Tian-Lu (李 天 祿 1910 ~ 1998). Prior to the film's release, Li, Tian-lu had already gained international fame and was invited to the 1988 Charleville Festival in France as a guest. The film helped elevate the recognition and appreciation for the art of hand puppetry in Taiwan. Because Hand Puppetry now incorporates a mix of art, literature, music, animation, and creativity, it renders endless possibilities to showcase Taiwanese culture on stage.

9.4 溫泉

••

　　臺灣的地理位置位於二大板塊的交界處，並在太平洋的地震帶上方，板塊的擠壓形塑出臺灣地區的多處山脈，也帶來了豐富的地熱與溫泉資源。早在日據時代，臺灣的溫泉資源就被發掘，經過殖民時期的開發，在全臺各處都有留下溫泉的據點，而日本文化中很重要的泡湯文化，也因此在臺灣留存下來。

　　臺灣目前已有超過 120 個溫泉湧泉處，全國各地皆有，北部著名的溫泉有北投、陽明山、烏來、礁溪，中部有谷關、泰安，南部有關仔嶺、知本，東部有瑞穗。全臺各處的溫泉，因為地質的不同，泉水內蘊涵的礦物質也不盡相同，總共有超過十種以上的泉質：碳酸氫鈉泉、白磺泉、青磺泉、鐵磺泉、硫磺泉、碳酸鹽泉、鹼性碳酸泉、海底溫泉、泥漿溫泉、氯化物碳酸氫鹽泉（海洋溫泉）、硫酸鹽氯化物泉。每種泉質對身體的療效也都不一樣，譬如弱鹼性碳酸泉，具有去角質及促進新陳代謝的功效，泡完能讓皮膚淨滑柔細，素有「美人湯」的稱號。硫磺泉帶有強烈的硫磺味，對改善神經痛、肌肉痠痛有幫助。泥漿溫泉因夾帶著地下岩層的泥質與豐富的礦物質，對皮膚病、風濕、關節炎特別有舒緩的療效。

　　現代人工作生活步調緊湊，即便不談溫泉的實際療效，光是作為單純的休閒娛樂，泡湯帶來的樂趣與舒緩效果，都是值得一試的，也因為如此，全臺各地才會持續不斷地開發新的溫泉勝地，提供大眾休閒的好去處。

Thermal Valley in Beitou, Taipei

9.4 Hot Springs

According to the Taiwan Tourism Bureau, Taiwan is ranked among the top 15 hot springs sites globally, having a high concentration and a good variety of hot springs throughout the island. With more than one hundred twenty hot springs discovered so far, one can find natural hot springs in virtually every county. Positioned in the Pacific Ring of Fire, Taiwan is located near a collision zone between the Yangtze Plate and the Philippine Sea Plate. Its unique geological position causes volcanic activities under the sea that produce subterranean heat and high-temperature springs across the island.

During Japanese colonial rule from 1895 to 1945, hot springs in Taiwan had been discovered and further developed into spas and resorts. Beitou (北投) is one such district in Taipei where many hot springs places came into existence during the Japanese era and are still in operations today. Famous hot springs in northern Taiwan are Beitou (北投), Jiaoxi (礁溪), Wulai (烏來), and Yangmingshan (陽明山); Guguan (谷關) and Tai'an (泰安) in central Taiwan; Guanziling (關子嶺) and Zhiben (知本) in southern Taiwan; Ruisui (瑞穗) in eastern Taiwan, just to name a few.

Hot springs are said to have many therapeutic effects. The high-temperature springs help increase the blood circulation within the body once soaked in the springs' waters. The mineral-rich water also helps fight arthritis, eczema, or chronic fatigue, in addition to a few other ailments. Contingent upon the type of mineral in the water, there are various springs in Taiwan, including sodium carbonate springs, sulfur springs, ferrous springs, sodium hydrogen carbonate springs, and salt or hydrogen sulfide springs. There is a further breakdown of the sulfur springs. Blue sulfur springs are particularly suitable for people with skin diseases, while white sulfur springs are recommended for people troubled by arthritis. Springs containing ferrous sulfide, moreover, can help ease muscle inflammation or nerve conditions. But sulfuric springs generally carry a distinctive scent due to their chemical nature.

In addition to hot springs, cold springs are also a signature natural water for which Taiwan is famous. In fact, cold springs are so rare that they are found only in Italy and Taiwan thus far. Su'ao (蘇澳) in eastern Taiwan is the place where Japanese troops discovered the natural cold springs in 1928. With temperatures hovering around 21 degrees Celsius all year round, a person immersing oneself in a cold spring will experience a bone-chilling freeze. However, because the springs are carbonated water rich in carbon dioxide, bubbles that cling to and tickle the body would stimulate the bather's blood circulation. Specifically, one should submerge the body into the cold springs up to waist level at first. Once the body has adjusted to the water temperature, sink further so that the water is up to one's neck. After a few minutes, the body would start warming up due to the invigorated blood circulation enabled by the cold springs' carbon dioxide frizz. Some people couldn't handle the coldness of the springs at first and would start paddling in the water. But this would actually interrupt the stimulation process and is not advised. Soak in the cold spring enough time to let it work its wonders.

Finally, in southern Taiwan, Guanziling (關 子 嶺) has the unique mud springs, discovered by Japanese troops in 1920 during their colonial rule, and is one of the few mud springs in the world. Mud springs contain minerals such as alkaline and iodine and are therapeutic in soothing skin irritations. Women enjoy applying the muddy water onto their skin as facials during the mud bath and, after which, would feel refreshed. The springs are also rich in methane - a natural gas - which creates the rare scene of a burning fire amidst spring water gushing out from underground. The co-existence of fire and water has been a famous tourist spot in southern Taiwan for centuries.

Wulai – a popular hot springs location near Taipei

Hot springs for relaxation

9.5 新衝浪天堂

　　臺灣的東海岸是岩岸地形，東邊的太平洋帶來很豐沛的浪潮，這些年來已成為衝浪者的新去處。2008 年及 2011 年連續二個國際衝浪盛事在東臺灣的臺東舉辦，吸引了世界各地的衝浪好手。亞洲衝浪錦標賽因此將臺灣入列為新的比賽地點，緊追馬來西亞、印尼峇里島、泰國之後。雖然臺東作為國際賽事的比賽場地，周邊的設施與條件仍有許多努力的空間，但先天的硬體條件如海浪品質、氣候溫度、天然景觀都讓臺東具備了極佳的潛力，成為亞洲的新衝浪天堂。

2019 Taiwan Open of Surfing (Courtesy of the Tourism Bureau in Taiwan)

9.5 Surfing Paradise

Taiwan is located in the Pacific Ocean with the Philippines to the south, Japan to its northeast, China to its west, and the vast Pacific Ocean to its east. The east Coast of Taiwan boasts a beautiful coastline with a breathtaking view of the Pacific Ocean. It is also blessed with abundant coral reefs that produce quality waves in size and shape. Autumn and winter seasons generally pick up big waves when the northeast monsoon blows. Due to these geographical features, Taiwan has become, in recent years, one of the hot new surfing spots in the world, dubbed the "new Hawaii."

In 2008, the inaugural East Coast International Surfing Competition drew international surfers from Australia and Indonesia to Taitung, Taiwan. Donghe County (東河鄉) in Taitung is a small fishing village and may not seem like a surfing mecca, but it consistently picks up the best waves on the entire east Coast of Taiwan. Only the experienced surfers are attracted to Donghe; however, the lack of infrastructure and its rocky beaches may not be surfer-friendly. Another nearby town, Jinzun (金 樽), enjoys the same conditions as Donghe but has more infrastructure ready for international visitors. As such, the Taiwan Open of Surfing, an international event since 2011, is held every year in Jinzun, Taitung, designated by the Asian Surfing Championship (ASC) as a new surfing venue. Joining Malaysia, Bali, and Thailand, Taitung has become the sixth leg in Asia in the Open Champion series.

Riding the waves

The annual event provides international surfers an opportunity to further appreciate the beauty on the east Coast of Taiwan, drawing over 100 competitors from Japan, South Africa, Australia, and Canada. The natural scenery and the pollution-free ocean are considered a surfing paradise by surfers. In addition to integrating with the ASC, the event is also putting efforts into joining the Association of Surfing Professionals (ASP), the main governing body in professional competitive surfing, in hopes of offering public education and training local talents in the newly rising industry. Although the sport is still in its infancy in Taitung and proper facilities are gradually being established, there is no doubt that Taiwan has many attributes to be a great surfing destination!

9.6 平溪天燈節

　　每年正月十五元宵節舉行的天燈節，是新北市平溪一年一度的盛會，曾經被知名的探索頻道列為全世界「此生必去的 15 個慶典」之一。

　　天燈的最早起源是在三國時代，孔明發明了天燈，藉此傳遞戰時訊息。後來先人來臺灣，最初開疆闢土的艱困時期，如果遇到土匪到村落裡搶劫，會將老弱婦孺先行撤離到深山裡避難，由壯丁留守捍衛村落，等到一切平安後，便會點燃天燈告知深山裡的老幼可以回歸村落了。天燈因此成為報喜報平安的象徵，也成為日後祈福的媒介，現在每年的天燈節就是民眾向天祈福來年平安豐收的慶典活動。

　　因為天燈節遠近馳名，吸引國內外的觀光客湧入平溪施放天燈，每年都有上萬盞天燈冉冉上升，但熄滅後的天燈掉落田間及樹林間，帶來生態的汙染，可說是不良的示範。2016 年時，文化銀行創辦人邵璦婷研發了環保天燈，使用紙漿等環保素材製作天燈，讓天燈可以在空中完全燃燒殆盡，不會在掉落時造成環境汙染，這項發明為天燈的設計帶來新的可能，也為天燈節向大地祈福的精神帶來嶄新的涵義。

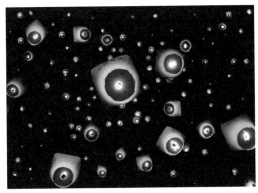

Lighting up the sky (Courtesy of David Yu)

Setting a sky lantern (Courtesy of David Yu)

9.6 Sky Lantern Festival

The Pingxi Sky Lantern Festival, held annually in Pingxi (平溪), New Taipei City on the 15th day of the first month of the lunar calendar, is considered the second largest carnival in the world by the Discovery Channel[1] (Taiwan Today, 2016). It has also been named by Fodor's as one of the *15 Festivals to Attend Before You Die* (Wasserman, 2016). Visitors gather every year during the Chinese New Year in the small town of Pingxi to attend the event. More than 100,000 lanterns will be launched midair and light up the night sky during the 3-day celebration.

Sky lanterns originated from the Three Kingdoms Period (220 CE ~ 280 CE), a historical period in which there were a lot of political unrest and military power struggles. During this period of political and social turmoil, a chancellor named Zhuge Liang (zhū gé liàng 諸葛亮) (181 CE ~ 234 CE) invented the unique lanterns to deliver military messages. As Zhuge Liang was also nicknamed Kongming (kǒng míng 孔明), these lanterns were also called Kongming lanterns. In 1821, when settlers migrated from China to the Pingxi area in Taiwan during the Qing Dynasty, villagers were often vulnerable to bandits' attacks after the harvest season. They would hide in the mountains with sufficient supplies, leaving only a handful of strong men to protect their villages. Once the worst of the winter was over, the remaining villagers would release sky lanterns to notify villagers in the

---

1　Pingxi lantern festival praised by National Geographic. (2016, January 15). *Taiwan Today.* Retrieved from https://taiwantoday.tw/news.php?unit=10,23,10&post=21671

Launching sky lanterns (Courtesy of David Yu)

hideout to return. Locals believed that the lanterns signify good luck and reunion. The once functional practice later evolved into the ritual of releasing sky lanterns to wish for prosperity and bountiful harvests.

Sky lanterns are traditionally made with a frame of bamboo strips, preferably from makino bamboo (guì zhú 桂竹), whose name is a pun for "prosperity" in Mandarin and therefore symbolizes "auspiciousness." The frame is then covered by four or five sides of rice paper, each of which can be written with a wish or invocation. A triangular wire piece is fixed at the bottom of the lantern to hold oil-soaked joss paper which functions as a wick. Once the joss paper is lit, hot air will soon fill up the lantern and allow it to fly into the sky.

A rising sky lantern

As the number of visitors at the Pingxi Sky Lantern Festival grows each year, concerns over the environmental impact of releasing thousands of lanterns may have grown stronger. The waste problem, despite beautiful images associated with sky lanterns, has always been a haunting issue. In 2016, a young entrepreneur named AiTing Shao (邵瓔婷) (Taiwan Scene, 2019) developed an eco-friendly sky lantern prototype entirely made from

Pingxi Sky Lantern Festival

paper. The traditional sky lanterns are usually made of water-resistant paper over bamboo frame and iron wire, all of which could get caught on the trees and hard to decompose. The eco-friendly lanterns, on the other hand, are made entirely from paper which is also used as fuel. Without the traditional components, eco-friendly lanterns can burn out in the sky at a certain altitude. Such an environmentally friendly invention makes it possible to host the *Sustainable Sky Lantern Festival* in Pingxi by civic groups, using lanterns that will burn up in the sky without a trace.

As Taiwan welcomes more visitors to experience the beautiful Sky Lantern Festival in Pingxi, there is hope that the environmentally friendly lanterns would carry the same well-wishing spirit that the cultural practice started with, only this time it is for Mother Earth.

References
參考書目與資料

- 台灣宗教巡禮 . (2017, May 11). *National Religion Information Network 全國宗教資訊網* . Retrieved from
  https://religion.moi.gov.tw/ChartReport/Index?ci=1&cid=2

- Anderson, G. H. (Ed.). (1998). *Biographical dictionary of Christian missions*. New York, NY: Macmillan Reference. Retrieved
  from http://bdcconline.net/en/stories/junius-robertus

- Cabinet approves budget for 'i-Taiwan 12' projects. (2009, November 27). *The China Post*. Retrieved from https://chinapost.nownews.com/20091127-122153

- Chang, D. (2017, July 12). Bubble tea: How did it start? *CNN Travel*. Retrieved from
  https://edition.cnn.com/travel/article/bubble-tea-inventor/index.html

- Charette, R. (2020, October 12). The original inhabitants of the island. *Taiwan Everything*.
  Retrieved from https://taiwaneverything.cc/2020/10/12/indigenous-tribes/#Amis

- Chi, C.-W. (2019, May). Behind Taiwan's same-sex marriage law, the 30-year crusade, *Common Wealth*. Retrieved from https://english.cw.com.tw/article/article.action?id=2410

- Crook, S. (2018, October). Holy conflagrations: Boat burnings at Taiwan's King Boat Festival. *Taiwan Scene: Formosa Tourism Journal*. Retrieved from https://taiwan-scene.com/holy-conflagrations-boat-burnings-at-taiwans-king-boat-festival/

- Crook, S. & Hung, K. H.-W. (2018). *A culinary history of Taipei: Beyond pork and Ponlai*. London, UK: The Rowman & Littlefield Publishing Group, Inc.

- Eight questions with the creators of Taiwan's first-ever eco-friendly sky lantern. (2019, August 31). *Taiwan Scene: Formosa Tourism Journal*. Retrieved from https://taiwan-scene.com/8-questions-with-the-creators-of-taiwans-first-ever-eco-friendly-sky-lantern/

- Felter, C. & Renwick, D. (2020, June). Same-sex marriage: Global comparisons. *Council on Foreign Relations Newsletter*. Retrieved from https://www.cfr.org/backgrounder/same-sex-marriage-global-comparisons

- Harper, K. (2018, March 19). The ancient art of fortune telling in a modern megacity. *Arts & Culture*. Retrieved from https://www.imb.org/2018/03/19/ancient-art-fortune-telling-modern-megacity/

- Intangible Cultural Heritage, United Nations Educational, Scientific, and Cultural Organization (UNESCO). (2009). *Mazu belief and customs*. Retrieved from https://ich.unesco.org/en/RL/mazu-belief-and-customs-00227

- Kellenberger, C. (2016, February 27). The legacy of George Leslie Mackay. *Canadian Chamber of Commerce in Taiwan*. Retrieved from https://canchamtw.com/the-legacy-of-george-leslie-mackay/

- Liu, A. C. (2009). *Taiwan A to Z: The essential cultural guide*. Taipei, Taiwan: The Community Services Center.

- Liu, J. (2014, April 4). Religious diversity index scores by country. *Pew Research Center*. Retrieved from https://www.pewforum.org/2014/04/04/religious-diversity-index-scores-by-country/

- Lu, K.-C. & Cheng, J. (2015, August 16). Taiwanese orchids to bloom in desert countries. *Common Wealth*. Retrieved from https://english.cw.com.tw/article/article.action?id=208

- MacKay, G. L. (2011). *From far Formosa: The island, its people and missions*. In J. A. MacDonald (Ed.). First edition printed in 1896, Digital print in 2011. New York, NY: Cambridge University Press.

- Number of convenience stores in Taiwan up almost 5% in 2019. (2020, August 7). *Focus Taiwan: CNA English News*. Retrieved from https://focustaiwan.tw/business/202008070007

- Paczek, T. (2017, April 10). Taiwan's musical garbage trucks lead the way in sustainability. *Facility Management*. Retrieved from https://www.fmmedia.com.au/sectors/taiwan-musical-garbage-trucks/

- Peng, C.H. 彭執瑄 (2016, January 8). Taiwan's religious diversity is a model of tolerance. *Taiwan Corner*. Retrieved from https://taiwancorner.org/?p=1985

- Pingxi lantern festival praised by National Geographic. (2016, January 15). *Taiwan Today*. Retrieved from https://taiwantoday.tw/news.php?unit=10,23,10&post=21671

- Quartly, J. (2016, July 15). The way of the gods – folk religion in Taiwan. *Taiwan Business Topics*. Retrieved from https://topics.amcham.com.tw/2016/07/the-way-of-the-gods/

- R.O.C. (Taiwan) Executive Yuan, Council for Economic Planning and Development. (2010). *Economic development, R.O.C. (Taiwan)*. Retrieved from https://ws.ndc.gov.tw/Download.ashx?u=LzAwMS9hZG1pbmlzdHJhdG9yLzEwL3JlbGGZpbGUvNTYwNy83MzIvMDAxNzUwOV8xLnBkZg%3D%3D&n=MjAxMl%2FntpPlu7rmnINf6Ie654Gj55m85bGV6lux5paH55Wr5YaKX%2BeAj%2BimvS5wZGY%3D&icon=..pdf

- ROC ranks 2nd in religious diversity index. (2014, April 17). *Taiwan Today*. Retrieved from https://taiwantoday.tw/news.php?unit=10&post=20619

- Rodgers, G. (2019, May 3). Overview of Taipei 101 tower. *TripSavvy*. Retrieved from https://www.tripsavvy.com/taipei-101-tower-facts-1458242

- Rossi, M. (2019). How Taiwan has achieved one of the highest recycling rates in the world. *Smithsonian Magazine*. Retrieved from https://www.smithsonianmag.com/innovation/how-taiwan-has-achieved-one-highest-recycling-rates-world-180971150/

- Severns, C. (2021, March 6). The development of the four Asian tigers. *Borgen Magazine: Humanity, Politics, & You*. Retrieved from https://www.borgenmagazine.com/development-of-the-four-asian-tigers/

- Taiwan top-ranked country in Asia for gender equality. (2019, February 18). *Focus Taiwan: CNA English News*. Retrieved from http://focustaiwan.tw/news/asoc/201902180013.aspx

- Taiwan's transition – from garbage island to recycling leader. (2019, June 18). *Rapid Transition Alliance*. Retrieved from https://www.rapidtransition.org/stories/taiwans-transition-from-garbage-island-to-recycling-leader/

- The joys of divination in Taipei. (2012, January 5). *Discover Taipei*. Retrieved from https://paper.udn.com/udnpaper/POH0056/209047/web/

- United Nations Development Programme, Human Development Reports. (2020). *Gender inequality index*. Retrieved from http://hdr.undp.org/en/composite/GII

- Wasserman, E. (2016, September 19). 15 festivals to attend before you die. *Fodors Travel*. Retrieved from https://www.fodors.com/news/arts-culture/15-festivals-to-attend-before-you-die

- Wroe, N. (2016, April 23). Cloud Gate: making dance out of martial arts and meditation. *The Guardian*. Retrieved from https://www.theguardian.com/stage/2016/apr/23/cloud-gate-taiwan-dance-song-wanderers

- Wu, F. (2018, June 14). The Mazu pilgrimage experience. *Common Wealth*. Retrieved from https://english.cw.com.tw/article/article.action?id=1985

國家圖書館出版品預行編目資料

Focal Point Taiwan: Formosan Snapshots
用英語說臺灣文化：浮光掠影話臺灣 / 崔正芳（Cynthia Tsui）編著
-- 初版 -- 臺北市：瑞蘭國際，2022.02
216 面；17 × 23 公分 --（繽紛外語；107）
ISBN：978-986-5560-57-7（平裝）

1.CST：英語 2.CST：讀本 3.CST：臺灣文化

805.18   110022624

繽紛外語系列 107

Focal Point Taiwan: Formosan Snapshots
用英語說臺灣文化：浮光掠影話臺灣

編著者｜崔正芳（Cynthia Tsui）
審訂｜徐鎝（Ruth Hsu）
責任編輯｜鄧元婷、王愿琦、潘治婷
校對｜崔正芳（Cynthia Tsui）、鄧元婷、王愿琦

視覺設計｜劉麗雪

瑞蘭國際出版
董事長｜張暖彗・社長兼總編輯｜王愿琦
編輯部
副總編輯｜葉仲芸・主編｜潘治婷
設計部主任｜陳如琪
業務部
經理｜楊米琪・主任｜林湲洵・組長｜張毓庭

出版社｜瑞蘭國際有限公司・地址｜台北市大安區安和路一段 104 號 7 樓之一
電話｜(02)2700-4625・傳真｜(02)2700-4622・訂購專線｜(02)2700-4625
劃撥帳號｜19914152 瑞蘭國際有限公司
瑞蘭國際網路書城｜www.genki-japan.com.tw

法律顧問｜海灣國際法律事務所　呂錦峯律師

總經銷｜聯合發行股份有限公司・電話｜(02)2917-8022、2917-8042
傳真｜(02)2915-6275、2915-7212・印刷｜科億印刷股份有限公司
出版日期｜2022 年 02 月初版 1 刷・定價｜480 元・ISBN｜978-986-5560-57-7
　　　　　2023 年 02 月初版 2 刷

瑞蘭國際